Sudden Tears

Suddenly, Phoebe was aware tears were running down her cheeks. She didn't bother to wipe them away. She knew she looked awful when she cried, but she didn't care. All she cared about was that the guy she loved and trusted had let her down.

"Wait a minute!" Griffin exclaimed. "I don't believe this. You mean you thought I didn't call you because I was with Sarah? That's the girl who's the lead in *West Side Story*. She's an actress. I just met her. She gave the whole pile of us a ride back — "

"Back?" Phoebe rubbed her face against her shirt sleeve. "Back from where?" she asked suspiciously.

"Oh, Phoebe!" Griffin took her in his arms. She didn't hug him back. "Phoebe, I love you. Don't you believe that?"

Books in the **Couples** series:

COUPLES

BROKEN HEARTS

M. E. Cooper

BANTAM BOOKS
TORONTO · NEW YORK · LONDON · SYDNEY · AUCKLAND

BROKEN HEARTS
A Bantam Book/November 1986
Reprinted 1987

Produced by Cloverdale Press Inc.,
133 Fifth Avenue, New York, NY 10003, U.S.A.

ISBN 0-553-17365-0

Printed and bound in Great Britain by
Cox & Wyman Ltd., Reading

Chapter
1

Just like the flowers in Sasha Jenkins's back-
yard, everything in Phoebe Hall's life was
blooming all at once. Phoebe leaned back
against the wrought-iron railing of the brick steps
and stared dreamily at the pale drifts of late
cherry blossoms and magnolias. Strains of an
old Beatles tune floated out the townhouse window across the herb garden. Phoebe hummed
along with the music, swaying to the beat. Suddenly Woody Webster's voice, followed by peals
of laughter, rose above the din of the party
inside. Phoebe grinned and hugged her knees
closer to her chest. She was so glad her friend
Sasha had invited her and all the rest of the gang
to the come-as-you-are party. Her heart felt so
big and full of love for the whole world, she
thought it might burst open. She closed her eyes
and inhaled deeply. The night air was mild and
sweet, and it enveloped her like a shawl. Phoebe

knew it was going to be the best spring of her life.

When she opened her eyes Griffin was standing there, holding two cans of soda. The breeze ruffled his brown hair, and in the dim light Phoebe could just make out the white letters on his I Love New York sweat shirt. He was looking down at her, a tender smile playing across his mouth.

He set down the sodas and said softly, "You look so beautiful."

Phoebe laughed self-consciously. "Like this?" She held out the sides of her oversized gray cardigan. It came down to her knees, and had a hole in the left elbow.

"Phoebe Hall! Are you daring to criticize my best sweater?" Griffin pulled her to her feet and close to him. He gently tugged her thick red hair. He gazed intently into her sparkling green eyes.

"Of course, if you like it that much, I'll wear it to the prom!" Phoebe teased.

"Perfect! That would be just perfect." Griffin threw back his head and laughed, then bent low to kiss her. She responded passionately, until she had to break away to catch her breath. Rubbing her cheek against his chest, she whispered, "Oh, Griffin, I'm so glad you're home at last. I really am."

Griffin tilted her face toward his and kissed her, at first gently, then more and more intensely on the mouth. Phoebe hugged him fiercely, as if pressing so closely together could close up all the distance that had been between them since last fall. She knew she could never bear his leaving again.

2

Suddenly Phoebe felt her feet lifted off the ground; Griffin was spinning her around and around in a circle.

"Put me down! Put me down!" she shrieked. But Griffin just spun her faster and faster across the yard. As he came to a stop, he murmured, "I love you so much, Phoebe."

When she sat down on the grass the yard was still spinning crazily in front of her eyes. She flopped onto her back and looked up. All the stars were swirling through the sky.

Griffin retrieved the sodas and plopped himself down, tailor fashion, next to her. They sat there knee-to-knee, against the gnarled old oak, catching their breath.

"This party was a great idea. I loved meeting your parents and all. Still. . . ." Griffin's voice trailed off. Phoebe squeezed his hand. She understood.

Not that anything had actually gone wrong between Griffin and her parents. When Griffin turned up unexpectedly in the middle of dinner, her mom simply set another place, heaped a plate full of chicken paprika, and set it in front of him with a warm smile. Griffin instantly liked her mom, Phoebe could see that. And her pesky younger brother, Shawn, didn't bother him at all. Shawn had hung on Griffin's every word, and made him tell the story of watching a Broadway magic show from the wings twice before dinner was over. But Phoebe could tell that her dad, though polite and nice enough, obviously had his doubts about her high-spirited friend from the

3

theatrical world. Phoebe told herself it was all Brad Davidson's fault.

Her old boyfriend, Brad, was just the kind of guy a parent loved to see a daughter date. He was handsome, considerate, and very smart. And at seventeen, had his whole life mapped out! He'd go to Princeton for pre-med and become a doctor like his dad and his dad's dad before him.

Phoebe had gone with Brad for two years, but last fall he had begun to drive her crazy with his neat little way of looking at the world. She knew her boyfriend better than she knew herself. Who was the real Phoebe Hall, anyway? What did she want to do with her life? Phoebe hadn't been quite sure then, but she knew that she loved to sing and harbored secret dreams of being an actress. An unplanned audition for Woody's Kennedy Follies led her straight into the arms of Griffin Neill, with whom she had sung a duet. The day after the Follies she broke up with Brad. Two days later Griffin left town to try out for a Broadway show.

Phoebe trailed her finger through a pile of blossoms and sighed softly. Sitting next to Griffin like this made last winter seem like a bad dream — lots of bad dreams, really. Lately, she wasn't sure which had been worse: losing Griffin for so many months, or trying to salvage what was left of her friendship with Brad. At one point she had even wondered if she had made a really big mistake leaving him. With Brad moping around Kennedy High, obviously still in love with her, and Griffin sending all sorts of mixed messages from New York, Phoebe had been tempted to try to make things work again with Brad. But then Brad fell in love with Brenda Austin, and finally, things began sorting themselves out in her long-distance relationship with Griffin.

Griffin scooped up a fistful of petals and tossed them at her. "Tell me about the prom. I've never been to one. Aren't I supposed to buy flowers to match your dress?"

Phoebe giggled. "That's the right idea. Except for one small problem."

"What's that?" Griffin flung himself down on his back, resting his head in Phoebe's lap. He could barely make out her pretty face in the dark. He closed his eyes a minute, as if to reassure himself that being home wasn't a dream after all. When he opened them she was still there. He smiled up at her.

"I don't have a dress yet. I'll get one tomorrow, after the audition, while I still have the car," Phoebe said.

Griffin frowned. "After the audition? You mean you were planning to come with me?"

"Of course!" Phoebe leaned back on her hands and grinned in the dark. "I can't wait, I'll finally get to see you in a real theater, on a real stage. I've never been to a professional audition, or met a famous director. My theatrical experience is limited to Woody's Follies. I sure didn't get much of a chance to watch you then." Phoebe smiled a little nostalgic smile and began to hum the tune to the duet she and Griffin had sung at the Follies.

Griffin sat up abruptly and started raking his hands through his hair. "Listen, Pheeb, I appreciate you wanting to give me a ride downtown and all. But it's okay, I can get there on my bike."

"Don't be silly. I already asked Mom for the car. I want to do this for you, Griffin, I really do." Phoebe squeezed his arm. His muscles felt all tense. "Griffin — is something wrong?" Phoebe asked hesitantly.

Griffin gave a low whistle under his breath. "I didn't think this would get so complicated. Nothing's wrong. I . . . I just have to be alone."

"Alone?"

"Oh, Phoebe, try to understand. If I wanted anyone to go to an audition with me, I'd want you. But, I don't know why exactly, it's just the kind of thing I need to do alone — on my own. I need quiet beforehand, time to get my head into the right place."

"I'd be real quiet. I don't have to say a word. I'd sit all the way in the back of the theater when we got there." Phoebe managed a feeble laugh. Griffin just had to be joking. Anyone she knew would want a friend along for an audition — certainly his best friend! If she was going to an audition she'd want Chris Austin, or Woody, or, above all, Griffin, to give her support, to give her someone familiar to sing to out there in the dark auditorium.

"I'm serious about this!" Griffin said firmly. She couldn't see his features in the dark yet, but his deep voice was so expressive. She knew exactly how he looked now — intense, passionate, very determined. Phoebe's heart stopped. He wasn't kidding. He didn't want her to go to the Arena Stage with him.

6

"I can't believe this." Phoebe swallowed hard. A lump was forming in her throat. "I just thought you'd want me there. It's not such a crazy thing to think." Phoebe couldn't go on. She held her palms against her forehead to press back the tears. She turned her head away from Griffin.

Instantly, Griffin was crouched down on the ground beside her. "Oh, Phoebe. I didn't know it would mean so much to you to come along." He stroked Phoebe's bowed head, his fingers toying with her thick tangled curls. "Pheeb, please try to understand. This has nothing to do with my feelings for you. It's just that a lot's changed for me since I went to New York. I learned so much there. You don't just walk into an audition; you prepare for it. It's like a real role. I figured the long morning bike ride to the theater would help me stay loose, and let me get my head together. If I were with you, well, all I'd think about is you. You know that." His hand trembled slightly as he turned her face toward his. Phoebe kept her eyes lowered.

She knew Griffin wanted her to meet his eyes, to smile, to say everything was okay. With all her heart Phoebe wished she could, but suddenly she felt very scared, and very alone — as if Griffin had never really come home. A lot *had* changed for him in New York, she had noticed that. He looked different, but she wasn't exactly sure how. His eyes didn't twinkle quite as they used to, and he seemed a little subdued. But that didn't bother her, it just made her want to be with him more, to help make the hurt and disappointment he had felt all winter go away.

It was this other thing that scared her, the feeling that Griffin's going to the audition alone was the first step of a journey she couldn't be part of — no matter how close to each other they got. It felt as though he were leaving her behind, again.

Griffin sat back on his heels and held her hands between his. "Phoebe, I love you very much, but there are some things a person has to do on his own."

She inhaled deeply and closed her eyes. When she had first met Griffin what she loved most about him was his free spirit, his independence, his unexpectedly crazy way of doing things, and the way he took risks. Until she met him she had never taken a risk in her life — not a big one. She wasn't sure why not going with him to the theater felt like a risk, but it did. She pressed her hands against her temples. Why did being in love feel like this? One minute her whole world was perfect and right, and so full of promise, as if nothing could ever really hurt her again. The next minute the perfect picture had fallen apart, and her heart was aching.

All at once she remembered the corny sixties poster of a bird Sasha's mother had in the kitchen: a stylized drawing of a hand letting go of a sparrow or swallow, Phoebe didn't know which. But she had always wondered at the words scrawled in pink paint across the pale sky. Something about letting what you love go free — not holding on too tight. Going to the audition tomorrow with Griffin had been her dearest wish, mainly so she could be with him as much as possible. After all, he had only just come back into her life.

She opened her eyes and sought Griffin's. "If that's how it's got to be . . . I guess I really wanted to see you on stage. . . ."

A sigh of relief escaped from Griffin's lips. Phoebe's strong reaction had taken him by surprise. He broke into a slow, teasing grin. "So that's the problem. You have your heart set on seeing me on a real stage. Phoebe Hall, you're going to get sick of seeing me on real stages. I intend to get that part tomorrow, and the next one I try for, and the one after that. And I expect you to be there every night, front row center, leading the applause. I'll play all my love scenes to you, until you're sick of me!"

"I'd never get sick of you." Phoebe shook her head solemnly, then wiped her cheeks with her fingers so Griffin wouldn't see the tear that had escaped from her eyes. Griffin's profile was so strong and handsome, even in the dark. He sounded so convincing. She giggled softly. "Sometimes, Neill, you can be so dramatic!" The smile quickly left her face. She took his arm and made him look into her eyes. "But promise you'll call right after the audition. Whatever happens. I'll be home waiting."

"Are you kidding?" Griffin pulled Phoebe to her feet and hugged her. "You'll be the first to know. Anyway, you're the one who's being dramatic. Just because I need to do some things alone, there's a lot more I want to do with *you*." Griffin kissed Phoebe, until the cold scary feeling she had that he was leaving her behind drifted off to a distant corner of her mind.

9

Chapter 2

"So, what do you think! Tell me — the truth, though." Phoebe swirled around once in front of the dressing room mirror.

Brenda Austin wrinkled her delicate nose. "It looks more like Sasha than you. I never did like mauve with red hair. I think you should get something black."

"Not the dress!" Phoebe wailed. "I mean, what do you think about Griffin? Last night's party was the first time you really got a chance to be with him. Wasn't he great when he sang 'Lullaby of Broadway'?" Phoebe caught her breath slightly at the memory. They had come in from the garden, and Woody dragged them over to the old upright and began banging out tunes from *Forty-Second Street*. Griffin's arm had stolen around her as they stood near each other at the piano, and he looked into her eyes as they started harmonizing in a duet. It was just like the first time they had sung together all over again. Suddenly, it almost didn't matter to her that she was not going with him to the audition.

Phoebe gave her head an impatient shake. She had promised herself, no moping today over what might have been. She was out with Chris and Brenda, getting a late start on the fun of shopping for the prom. Anyway, she was dying to know what everyone at the party had thought of Griffin.

Her large, green eyes turned imploringly from Brenda to Chris, who stood in the dressing room across the way, looking every inch the prom queen in a strapless white tulle gown with a pink rose at the waist. "Come on, you two, tell me. Did you like him?"

Chris Austin's classic features softened into a warm smile. "Oh, I don't know . . ." she began slowly, deliberately concentrating on holding her long blond hair up off her neck and studying the effect. "Brenda, are you sure this is the right dress for a prom with the theme springtime in Paris? I look so hopelessly all-American!"

Brenda glanced up sharply from unzipping Phoebe's dress. As she caught her sister's eye, the puzzled expression on her face gave way to a conspiratorial smile. "Chris, you *are* all-American. You can't help it. You were typecast at birth. I think that dress suits you fine. Don't you, Phoebe?"

Phoebe drew in her breath sharply. "Yes. Chris looks great! I thought we settled that fifteen minutes ago." She kicked her toe impatiently against the curled edge of the carpet. "But what about Griffin?"

"Not quite my type," Brenda said crisply, watching Phoebe step out of the yards of mauve net and lace. "Actors never are." She bent down, avoiding looking Phoebe in the eye.

"Oh," Phoebe said flatly. She couldn't stand it if her friends didn't like Griffin. She knew how hard things had been for her good friend Sasha when she had fallen for a guy from Kennedy's rival school.

Chris's laughter rippled across the hall. Letting her hair cascade back down her neck, she squeezed Phoebe's hand. "Brenda's kidding. So am I, I loved him. Everyone did. He's cute, and absolutely perfect for you."

"But the dress is not." Brenda hung the gown back on the pink, padded hanger and gave it an annoyed shake. She gave Phoebe a long, serious look. "What I liked about Griffin is he seems up front and honest. With a guy like that you'll always know where you stand. I like that — a lot. It must feel great having him back in Rose Hill again." Brenda turned and headed for the door, her arms full of rejected gowns. "But now back to business. Let me scout around one more time. Saks has to have the true Hall original. None of the other stores Chris and I tried last week had anything better. I think you're too hung up on looking like those silly prom pictures in *Seventeen*. This gauzy stuff just isn't your style."

Chris winced at her stepsister's words. Phoebe

12

watched her doubtfully finger the white tulle of her skirt and frown at her reflection in the mirror. As soon as Brenda was down the hall, Phoebe whispered, "Don't be so paranoid, Chris. Brenda didn't mean you, she meant me. She was right, that dress was too romantic for me. But the one you've got on is made for you, Chris Austin. Take it off and buy it."

Chris grinned sheepishly. "When it comes to Brenda, I still get too sensitive, don't I?"

"You've come a long way — you both have," Phoebe declared, helping Chris out of her dress. She was still amazed that over the course of the last few months the two stepsisters had really become friends, and had seemed to learn from each other in the process. Chris found it easier to laugh at herself these days, and Brenda wasn't so anti-everything. She was actually beginning to really fit in to the Kennedy scene.

Phoebe was never sure what the other kids actually thought of Brenda. For a long time, dark-haired, beautiful Brenda sure looked the part of bad-girl-on-campus. It had all been an act. Phoebe had always known that, and so had Chris. Fortunately, over the past few months Brenda had softened a great deal. The haunted, scared look in her eyes had practically vanished. What everyone had called hardness had proven to be a no-nonsense, straightforward approach to people. She wasn't very good at playing games and didn't like them. She might turn away from a difficult situation, or act rebellious and weird, but she'd never pretend everything was okay. That's what Brad loved about her, and why he needed her.

Phoebe could understand that now. Brad had always been as good as Phoebe at making believe everything was nice and rosy, when everything might actually be gray and dead. If it hadn't been for Brad teaming up with Brenda, Phoebe might have become good friends with Brenda sooner. Eventually, the awkward coolness between them had thawed. Phoebe was glad of that now. Especially when she looked up and saw the dresses Brenda carried back into the room for her.

"These are more like it, don't you think?" Brenda dumped the dresses on a chair, and pushed the dainty chain bracelet dangling from her wrist higher up on her arm.

"I don't know." Chris squinted skeptically at the bright taffeta gowns. "They sort of look like something Cyndi Lauper or Madonna might wear!"

"You said it!" Phoebe cried delightedly, touching first one then the other. "How could we miss these? They're practically neon! Where did you find them?"

"A couple of departments down in that new New York Boutique — definitely not on the junior rack for prom dresses. The saleswoman thought I was shoplifting when I brought them back here, of course," Brenda muttered tensely.

"That's *her* problem!" Chris declared vehemently. Brenda smiled shyly at her stepsister's loyalty. "Anyway," Chris continued, "I'll have to see them before I can believe anything like this is right for Pheeb." She fingered a bright green dress distastefully.

14

"How could you doubt it?!" Phoebe was already slipping into her favorite. It was almost strapless. The black clinging top had one broad pink and black taffeta strap over the right shoulder. The calf-length skirt had three broad flounces of alternate layers of bright pink and black taffeta. Phoebe faced the mirror and stared wide-eyed at her reflection. She sure didn't look like a prom queen. She looked more like a rock star. A goofy smile spread across her face. Griffin would love the dress. She looked so wild and dramatic. So stagey! She could picture the two of them now, walking into the gaily decorated gym. Griffin would be wearing the tall, black top hat he told her about last night. They'd look like one of those posters of turn-of-the-century Paris and the French cancan. What an entrance they'd make! Yes, this was the perfect dress. It made her feel so crazy and alive.

Abruptly the sparkle went out of her eyes. Here she stood grinning like an idiot in front of the mirror, at the very moment when the guy she loved was going through one of the toughest days of his life. Griffin's whole future was on the line, and she was imagining making a grand entrance at a high school prom.

"Pheeb, what's the matter?" Chris asked, watching the color fade from Phoebe's rosy cheeks. "Do you feel all right? Is something wrong with the dress? I have to admit I like it. Don't you?"

"Nothing's wrong," Phoebe lied. "I was just wondering. Is it too low-cut? Don't you think I'm too fat for something like this?"

"Fat!" Brenda scoffed. "You've got to be kidding. Half the kids I know would kill for a figure like yours. And it's definitely not too low-cut. It's no lower than Chris's gown."

Chris giggled. "I think what's worrying her is will Griffin like it."

"If he doesn't, he's got something seriously wrong with him." Brenda snorted.

Phoebe forced a smile. "Chris is right — I was worried about Griffin."

"How could he not like it? It looks very New York," Brenda said practically. "Anyway, from the way he was looking at you last night, I'd say whatever you decided to wear to the prom would make him happy, even your overalls."

"Really? You mean that?"

Brenda and Chris shrugged at each other. "What are we going to do with her?" Chris murmured, nodding toward her blushing friend.

"Beats me," Brenda said, helping Phoebe squirm out of the tight bodice. "But they did have a pair of orange satin overalls out there — "

Phoebe giggled. "Okay, you two, I get the message. Loud and clear. Griffin loves me. And he'll love the dress. That settles it. This is the dress I get. How much is it?" She blanched slightly as she glanced at the price tag. "Brenda, no wonder the saleswoman thought you were shoplifting. This is much more than my mom said I should spend." Phoebe calculated quickly in her head. She'd have to baby-sit every night for the next two months, including the night of the prom, to make up the difference. And her birthday wasn't until August 16. She had better figure

16

out something before her mom got the bill. "Thank goodness Mom gave me her charge card." She sighed as she pulled on her old pink overalls.

On her way back from Rezato, Laurie Bennington made two small detours.

Driving through the center of town, she passed Sasha's townhouse. She gave a small, self-satisfied grin at discovering Janie Barstow's old green Plymouth parked behind the Jenkins's Rabbit. She thought she had overheard the two of them in the ladies room at school talking about collaborating over the weekend on a pre-prom article for *The Red and the Gold*.

She made a right turn, then a quick left, and headed toward the mall. Sure enough, Henry Braverman's car was outside the sub shop. Her victorious smile quickly gave way to a perplexed frown. What was Phoebe's station wagon doing here? Wasn't this the big afternoon for her airhead actor boyfriend's audition? Phoebe must be crazy letting him go alone, she thought. If he were my guy, I wouldn't let him get that far out of my sight again.

But that was Phoebe's business. Laurie had her own business to attend to. She needed to corner Henry alone, right away. Her foray into Rezato had clinched it. The new, black-silk dress her father had brought back from Paris was beautiful, but it wasn't exactly what Laurie had in mind for the prom. Black silk would look all wrong when she was crowned prom queen. And anyway, it was too blatantly sexy for her new boyfriend Dick Westergard's taste. He liked softer-looking

17

clothes. Too bad she couldn't train her father to ask her in advance what she wanted him to bring back from Paris.

But she had found what she wanted anyway, at Rezato — one of Henry's crazy creations. She hated to admit it, but he really was going to be a great designer someday. In fact, he was already. Take that dress: Even on the hanger it was soft, elegant, and it draped like a dream. When she tried it on, it looked perfect, and she was pleased to discover it had a discreet, but very sexy, slit up the side — way up the side. Just one thing was wrong: the color, chrome yellow, the one color she looked crummy in. She had to find Henry and con him into making one to order. She'd pay him, of course. It should be red, or maybe a deep electric blue, to match the new Parisian Midnight cellophane rinse she had in her hair.

The trouble was she didn't want Janie to get wind of her plans. Laurie got the feeling Janie had never quite forgiven her for the problems she had caused about homecoming and Peter Lacey. If Janie saw Laurie with Henry she'd get all paranoid, and figure Laurie was trying to steal her guy. Last fall the idea not only would have been ludicrous — Henry seemed like a nerdy nobody back then — but it would have appealed to some crazy part of her. Now the thought of possibly hurting Janie made her feel kind of uncomfortable. Still, people weren't willing to let Laurie live down her old bad reputation. Not that she had to worry about that today. Janie wasn't around.

"Hi, gang!" Laurie bubbled to no one in particular as she pushed her way through the swinging glass doors. The guy Tony had hired as a new dishwasher looked up and whistled as Laurie swung by, her tight leather pants squeaking slightly as she walked. Laurie pointedly ignored him and stopped in the middle of the floor, scanning the room for Henry's lanky frame.

"Hi, Laurie," Chris called from the crowd's favorite corner booth. Laurie noticed two pink Saks boxes poking out from beneath Brenda's jean jacket on the seat. Chris and Brenda must have been shopping with Phoebe for a prom dress.

She wondered what they had managed to find in Saks. Only yesterday she had combed the store. Nothing seemed even vaguely interesting. Chris probably got one of those perfectly horrid little white gowns that looked like rejects from the bridal boutique.

It was hard to picture Brenda buying anything from Saks; she usually haunted those ratty downtown thrift shops, or some of the punk D.C. boutiques. So the other box must belong to Phoebe. She had probably gone and bought something gauzy and green. Laurie gave a little shrug; what the other girls wore didn't matter much. If her plans worked out with Henry, she'd be the best-dressed prom queen in the history of Kennedy High.

"Where's Henry?" Laurie asked, sliding into the booth next to Chris. She found herself staring across the table into Brenda's dark, suspicious eyes. She averted her glance and smiled at Phoebe.

"Haven't seen him since last night," Phoebe replied, waving part of one of Tony's super salami sinker subs toward Laurie. "Want some? I decided to have one last 'diet blaster,' before getting serious about being skinny in time for the prom."

"No way," replied Laurie with a toss of her head. "Dick and I are going to Georgetown for dinner tonight. So none of you have seen Henry?"

"Henry Braverman?" Chris asked, surprised that Laurie seemed so intent on seeing him. Chris had noticed that Laurie was nice enough in general to Henry and Janie these days. But when Henry had been put in charge of the prom decorations and planning, Laurie hadn't made a secret of the fact that she had expected to get the job. Even though, as Woody had quipped, she was about as artistic as an amoeba.

"As you can see, he's not around here," Brenda said sharply. "What do you want with him, anyway?"

None of your business, Laurie started to say, but she bit her lip and answered smoothly, "Prom business. I need to talk to him about stuff for the decorating committee — and other things. You know, posters from Paris, all the stuff my dad brought back."

"Maybe he's at Janie's," Phoebe suggested helpfully.

"I don't think so, I already saw Janie's car parked outside of Sasha's. Henry's car is here."

Chris laughed. "Laurie, someday you should

go into the detective business. So that's how you keep track of what's going on with who around town."

"Spy business is more like it," Brenda mumbled into her Coke.

Laurie glared daggers at Brenda and began absently shredding a napkin. For a few minutes no one said anything. Finally Laurie shrugged as if to say, what Brenda Austin thought of her wasn't very important, not in the long run.

Phoebe finally broke the silence. "Listen, everybody, I hate to break up the party. Especially since this pig-out was my bright idea. But Griffin's probably finished his audition by now, and I want to get home and find out how it went."

"I'm surprised you didn't go with him," Laurie commented, as Phoebe began wrapping up the remains of her sub to bring home to Shawn. "An audition at the Arena Stage is a pretty big thing for a seventeen-year-old — for anybody, actually. I pictured you there bravely standing by your man, as the song goes."

Phoebe paused before noisily stuffing the sandwich into a brown bag Chris had retrieved from the counter. "I could have gone, I guess," she said quickly, not meeting anyone's eyes. "But I had to get my dress. Next week will be too late. Until Griffin came back, I really didn't even intend to go to the prom."

Laurie squinted at her. Phoebe Hall was actually lying. Phoebe never lied, and she sure was crummy at it. Had she and Griffin had a fight already? He had only been back in town a couple of days.

"If I were Griffin, I wouldn't want Phoebe along at my audition," Brenda said as she slipped on her jacket.

"Come off it," Chris frowned. "Ted would want me along. Brad would want you. What Laurie said makes sense. I kind of wondered myself why you decided to go shopping with us today," she concluded, turning to Phoebe.

Phoebe lowered her eyes and grinned sheepishly. "To tell you the truth, Brenda's right — Griffin didn't want me to come." Her voice trembled slightly. "I — I can't say I liked staying behind, but shopping turned out to be fun. Did you really mean that, Brenda?"

"Sure, I couldn't concentrate on what I was supposed to be doing. I still have a hard time if Brad comes to Garfield House with me, and the other kids and I get into a rap session. It's a part of myself that's separate from him, that's all. I think it's smart for Griffin to have gone alone. Just because you're going together doesn't mean you have to do *everything* together."

Phoebe sighed a happy sigh and glanced up at the big, red clock. "Sorry to walk out on you like this, Laurie, but I really do have to get back. Not just for Griffin — " She added quickly, "I'm baby-sitting my favorite pesty brother tonight!"

"To each her own!" Laurie said skeptically. Phoebe was too innocent about these things, she thought. Laurie hadn't seen the mysterious Griffin since he had gotten back, but he wasn't acting like a guy who had been away from the girl he loved all winter long. Audition or no audition, he should want her by his side. Laurie knew Dick

22

would want her around, no matter what happened. And knowing that was the best feeling in the world.

"Hey, sugar, want a Coke? On the house?"

Laurie snapped out of her daydream. "No, thanks!" She sprang up and away from the lanky dishwasher who was leaning over the back of the booth, a disgusting-looking sponge in his hand.

Flinging her leather jacket over one shoulder, she stomped out of the sub shop, relieved to see Henry's car still parked in the half-empty lot. He had to be somewhere in the mall, and it didn't take a genius to figure out what was his favorite store. She could kick herself for having wasted so much time at the sub shop. She should have thought of the Fabric Mart first of all.

Chapter
3

Henry Braverman draped a length of the pale silk and linen fabric over his arm. Beneath the Fabric Mart's cool fluorescent lights, the material shimmered like champagne laced with gold — like Janie's hair last night. She had turned up at Sasha's party with a new asymmetrical haircut. Her fine brown hair had been subtly highlighted, and the long part that fell over one side of her high-cheekboned face had been streaked pale blond. Her wide-set hazel eyes had taken on the color of old, yellowed gold. The effect had been striking. Maybe he was prejudiced, but Henry felt she had been the most beautiful girl there.

Janie's prom dress just had to be made from this fabric. Henry shook his head doubtfully. The dress he pictured would be long, almost floor-length, with a tight bodice. And to continue the asymmetrical theme of Janie's hair, one side would be strapless. The other would have one sleeve. The design would require several yards of fabric. At nearly forty dollars a yard after his discount, he knew he couldn't afford it.

"Henry! Henry Braverman," a breathy voice cried behind him.

Henry looked up and squinted down the long empty aisle leading to the Fabric Mart's design studio alcove.

He nervously pushed his blond hair off his forehead as she walked up. "Laurie? What are you doing here?" She was one girl at Kennedy who definitely never made her own clothes.

"Looking for you!" Laurie smiled coyly.

His blue eyes narrowed slightly. Ever since last winter's fashion show, and the pushy number she had pulled on Woody, he hadn't trusted Laurie. Even though the other kids seemed to feel she had toned down her act and become more of a human being since she met Dick Westergard, he still felt hurt. And with good reason. He didn't feel like doing any favors for a girl who had been so mean to Janie. Anyway, her blatantly sexy fashion sense rather jarred him. Everything about her always seemed overdone.

Her good-natured laugh startled him. "Don't look so suspicious. I have a perfectly good reason for looking for you — goodness, what beautiful material." Laurie fingered the fabric as Henry carefully rolled it around the tall bolt. "I bet that costs a fortune."

"Pretty close to it," Henry admitted ruefully. He stepped a few feet away from Laurie. She was wearing a heavy perfume that made him want to sneeze.

25

"Actually I'm looking for you because I'd like to make a deal."

"A deal?"

"A business deal. I was over at Rezato and saw that great yellow dress of yours, and I decided I just had to have it for the prom."

Henry grimaced. "Yellow? You'd look dreadful in that — " He stopped himself and colored slightly. He hadn't meant to sound insulting.

Laurie surprised him. She wrinkled her nose and nodded agreement. "Precisely. That's why I'm looking for you. I know you said you weren't going to make any prom dresses, but couldn't you just — for me — please make that dress all over again. It fit perfectly. You could use the same pattern, but in a better color. Like red or blue, whatever you think would look good on someone like me. But not black," she added quickly.

Henry shook his head. "There's no time. I'm all tied up doing the decorations for the dance, and then I've got to make Janie's dress. I really can't, Laurie. I'm sorry."

Laurie frowned. Then her face brightened. "I'll pay you, of course, the same thing Rezato charges. That would only be fair. We could pick out the fabric now. It would only take a minute."

Henry started shaking his head, then he stopped thoughtfully. Rezato had the dress marked up to one hundred-fifty dollars. He never charged the kids in school what they would have paid retail. Still, lately he hadn't had time to design clothes for the girls, except Janie. He was too busy filling orders for Rezato, and now, a couple of boutiques up in Baltimore and in Philadelphia. But one hundred-fifty dollars would cover *exactly* what he needed to pay for the beautiful fabric for Janie's dress.

"I'll even pay extra for the fabric. I'll have to give you the money for the dress on Monday. But I have it, don't worry," Laurie declared.

Henry gritted his teeth and smiled. Like Laurie or not, he was going to have to go through with this. "Okay, I'll do it. It's a deal."

Laurie sighed happily. "Good. Now exactly what do you think is my best color?" Laurie scanned the display tables. Her eyes rested longingly on a bolt of red, silk crepe. Her hand stole to her hair, and she resolutely walked over to a cobalt-blue print.

Henry shook his head. "Red, not blue. You can always put a different rinse in your hair," he said in a firm, professional tone. "Not that red, either. It's wrong — too orangey, and the material won't fall correctly. Let's try over here."

Laurie obediently followed Henry, until he found something that suited them both.

After Laurie had paid for the fabric, Henry hurried off to Janie's house. Mrs. Barstow would help him cut it out this afternoon, in the basement workshop that he and Janie had set up. He could work on the dress tomorrow. And Laurie had promised to pay him Monday. This gave him plenty of time to make Janie's gown, too.

Halfway to his car he stopped abruptly. Was he crazy? He had already told Phoebe, and Chris, and the rest of the crowd he wasn't making anyone's dress but Janie's. Well, let them

27

think Laurie had bought it at the boutique. Janie probably wouldn't remember the dress he sold to Rezato was yellow. He'd have it finished quickly, and Janie wouldn't even know he had gone back on his word to their friends.

"Sasha, look at this!" Janie Barstow shoved a large oversized Italian fashion magazine across the window seat. She couldn't read a word of the copy, but the photographs and drawings were really incredible. She couldn't wait to give it to Henry. Her dad had brought a pile of slick foreign fashion monthlies back from a business trip to New York.

"Why, that model looks just like you!" Sasha said between bites of her carob-nut brownie.

"She does?" Janie tilted her head and studied the photo, then craned her neck to peer in the oval mirror above Sasha's dresser. The girl looking back at her in the reflection in no way resembled the Janie Barstow who had moved from Cincinnati to Rose Hill last year. Gone was the long, mousy-brown hair, the bangs hiding half her pale-skinned face. Even her eyes seemed to have changed color; they looked more gold now than the nondescript green they had been. It was as if a fairy godmother had waved a magic wand over her. Sasha was right. She did look a lot like the elegant model with the champagne and gold dress. But there had been no fairy godmother. Just Henry Braverman, and his fantastic dress designs. Henry said it wasn't just her new clothes that made her suddenly the envy of most of the girls at Kennedy. He said it was the way she walked and talked, and how she had come out of her closet of shyness. Clothes gave her the initial confidence, not to be a fashion queen, but to be herself. Janie blushed slightly as she looked into the mirror. She didn't know about confidence or clothes, but she was sure of one thing: She had found the perfect guy in Henry Braverman. And that had changed how she felt about her whole life, not just her appearance. "I guess I'm not used to myself in this haircut," she said with a shy smile.

"Not just the cut — " Sasha giggled, "— the color. You make an incredible looking blond! Maybe you should bleach your whole head sometime."

Janie shook her head solemnly. "No. I wouldn't like that. Henry wouldn't either. I know how he feels about extreme stuff. He likes it this way. Anyway, I didn't show you this picture, Sasha Jenkins, to see if I looked like a model. I thought this kind of thing was a great idea for the fashion column we were talking about last night."

Sasha knelt on the floor beside the window seat and studied the spread. "You mean the drawings. Henry could do those, and then you could write about what kids around Kennedy were wearing."

"Sure, that would solve the problem of pictures. That way, no one's feelings would be hurt. If we mentioned some trends are definitely out — Henry could do a quick sketch of someone with saggy kneesocks — and it wouldn't have to look like anybody in particular."

Sasha sat back on her heels and smiled warmly

at Janie. "I hadn't thought of that. But this kind of column could be used the wrong way. I don't want it to hurt people, or start feuds. Some of the trendy dressers around school could get pretty competitive over being included in a write-up or being left out. Let's try one right after the prom — maybe even using what people wore prom night as the theme. If it works we can make it into a regular feature next year."

"Good idea," Janie said. She abruptly leaped to her feet, then reached for her book bag. She settled down on the floor next to Sasha and began reviewing notes on a long, yellow pad. "But now we have to get down to prom business. We really need help with the decorations. Maybe it was a mistake for Henry to be made head of the decorations committee. He's so busy working on the art part, he hasn't been able to drum up enough people to help with canvassing stores for donations, and getting kids just to volunteer for stuff like blowing up balloons." She shrugged slightly and concluded, "Maybe Laurie should have gotten the job. At least all the guys on campus would have volunteered to help."

"To help with what?" Sasha quipped, then added loyally, "Henry is perfect, and so are you. The idea of painting Paris street scenes on fabric to decorate the gym walls is fabulous. I think we can drum up lots of interest through *The Red and the Gold*. First of all, I'll get this interview with you and Henry polished up tonight. That way it can go to press tomorrow, and it will give you tons of publicity."

"I almost forgot: Peter will be good for some

30

lunchtime pep talks on the radio," Janie added. "I spoke with him last night at the party. He's going to announce the prom queen candidates next week. That should wake people up a bit."

Sasha glanced quickly at Janie's face. She was bent over her notepad checking off items on her list. Sasha discreetly turned to the back of her notebook. The advance list of prom queen candidates Peter had given her at the party was still there. Janie hadn't seen it. Sasha had promised Peter not to show a soul, and to bring it to the printer herself the next day so word wouldn't leak out of the journalism room. Peter's announcement was going to wake a lot of people up — and send some of them into a state of shock.

Janie gnawed the end of her pencil, and smiled slyly at Sasha. "Who are you going to vote for? I mean the ones we know about already. I'm going to vote for Chris, of course."

"Plenty of time to think about that later. I am famished. Let's get more brownies downstairs before we head off to Georgetown to pick up my dress," Sasha said quickly. She didn't want to commit herself. Not yet. Anyway, she felt guilty that she had already seen the list. Usually, it would be Chris she'd vote for. But this year, she wasn't quite sure. Not that Chris didn't deserve it, but there was someone else as of late who had been looking positively chic.

Chapter
4

"Yankees seven, Orioles six, going into the bottom of the ninth, top of the order coming up to bat for the home team. Listen to that crowd, folks — they haven't given up yet. As the saying goes, 'It ain't over till it's over.' "

Phoebe wished fervently that it *was* over, and that the Yankees would win the game. She had gotten in the habit of rooting for New York teams during the winter. Shawn had even threatened to beat her up when she came back from visiting Griffin wearing a Yankees pinstriped T-shirt.

At the moment, however, it was Shawn who was cruising for a bruising. Baby-sitting benefits should include earplugs, or at least a Walkman that worked, she thought to herself. She jumped off the couch and roared down the stairs that led to the family room. "Shawn Hall! If you don't turn that TV down I'm going to shove your head through the screen!"

She waited a minute at the top of the stairs, tapping her foot. He probably couldn't hear her over the noise. She started to yell again, then stopped. Yelling just made her headache worse. She flopped back down on the sofa and buried her head beneath a couple of chintz throw pillows. She didn't care that her high-topped pink sneakers were on the new upholstery. She was in such a crazy mood that in some strange way, she relished the thought of doing something to make her mom angry.

The grandfather clock began to chime. Phoebe peeked from behind the cushions. It was already ten. Griffin hadn't called yet, and she was worried, angry, and ready to kick herself for waiting all night by the phone. It wasn't the first time he'd done this — not calling when he promised. But that was when he was down and out in New York. It was different now, he was back in Rose Hill. No matter how this audition went, he should want to tell her about it. Right away. She tossed one of the pillows across the floor. It landed in her dad's antique rocker.

Darn. She could have gone to the concert with her mom. Her father probably would have preferred watching the dumb game with Shawn. Then Chris and Ted had phoned and invited her, along with a bunch of other kids, to the Chesapeake Drive-In for a double bill of Phoebe's two all-time favorite horror flicks. Worse yet, she was stuck here at home and couldn't even watch

Love Boat, thanks to Shawn, the baseball game, and the broken living room TV.

Maybe Griffin had tried to call, she reasoned to herself, but the line was busy. She had kept her conversations short, but still, she had already chatted with Sasha and Chris. Or maybe something had happened to him — a bike accident in D.C. Phoebe sat up abruptly. Would his mom know to call her? She reached for the phone. Then she remembered no one had been home fifteen minutes ago, the last time she had tried his number.

"You call me or something?"

Phoebe threw her hands up in the air and glared at her brother. Looking at him, her face instantly softened into a smile. What a crazy kid. Standing there in his he-man T-shirt, with a baseball cap yanked down over his red, curly hair, he looked so lovably ridiculous. "Shawn, can't you turn down the volume just a notch?" she pleaded.

His freckled face wrinkled into a perplexed frown. "It's off. It's over. They lost." He sank into a disconsolate heap at the foot of the sofa and sighed. Phoebe didn't have to ask who won. And she had gotten so used to the racket from the basement, she hadn't even noticed the sudden silence.

"Hey, is something burning?" Shawn sniffed the air, and leaped to his feet.

"Oh, no!" Phoebe wailed. "Our brownies!" They tore into the kitchen. Plumes of smoke drifted out of the oven. A moment later she looked at the charred lump sitting in the black-

34

ened cake pan, and tears she hadn't been able to cry all night filled her eyes.

"It's not that tragic. After all, they weren't *real* brownies. They were your weird friend's non-chocolate recipe. Real brownies — that would be something to cry over," Shawn said practically.

Phoebe met Shawn's wide green eyes, and the two of them suddenly collapsed onto the kitchen chairs laughing. After they recovered, he suggested she send out for pizza.

"I only have two dollars. That's not enough for a pizza and a tip. We can't do it. Sorry, Shawn. Anyway, I'd better clean up this mess." She started to add, "And it's past your bedtime!" But he was already out of the room, yelling something about money.

Just as Shawn returned with his old piggy bank and the biggest hammer in the house, the doorbell rang.

"Oh, it's Griffin!" Phoebe dried her hands and ran into the front hall. She quickly fluffed out her hair and threw open the door.

"Pheeberooni! It smells like the house is on fire!"

Phoebe couldn't hide her disappointment. She tried to smile. "Woody, Kim, come on in. What are you doing here? Didn't you guys head down to the drive-in?"

Kim pulled off her scarf and sniffed the air. "Carob. Burnt carob. Isn't it vile? Is Sasha here?"

"No. Just one of Sasha's recipes. Actually, it's a good one. I tried it before, carob-walnut brownies, but I forgot I had them in the oven and — "

"And the fire department arrived in the nick of time." Woody kicked his feet into the air, snapped his red suspenders, and strode into the kitchen. "How ya doing, Shawn, old boy. Some game, wasn't it?"

"They lost."

"So you're going to take it out on your piggy bank?" Woody's voice drifted into the living room. Kim and Phoebe grinned knowingly at each other. Woody's kooky sense of humor appealed to Shawn.

"Did we come at a bad time?" Kim eyed Phoebe critically. "You didn't look too thrilled to see us standing on the other side of the door. We don't have to stay. We were just heading out for pizza after watching the game at my house, and we thought you'd like to come."

Phoebe shook her head and squeezed Kim's arm. "No. I'm glad you showed up. Just in the nick of time, too. I'm starved. Maybe we can order in for pizza. I can't leave."

"Baby-sitting?" Woody strolled out of the kitchen and plopped himself down in the big, old rocking chair, his long legs stretched out in front of him. The floorboards squeaked as he rocked. "Shawn tells me he was about to rob his piggy bank to feed the poor starving Hall kids." He paused to sip a Coke he had helped himself to from the refrigerator. "I rescued the poor critter. With the cost of college going up, you have to get your eight-year-olds in the habit of hoarding early. The pennies they save may be your own."

"Ooooh. Stop, Woody. I've got a headache," protested Phoebe with a smile.

"Malnutrition. That settles it. I'll phone Mario's. One large — the works."

"Why don't we just all hop in the car and take Shawn with us?" Kim suggested. "It'll be just as fast. Your folks wouldn't mind. After all, it's Saturday night, and Shawn doesn't have to be in bed at ten."

"You bet I don't!" Shawn yelled, grabbing his jacket from the hall closet. "Let's go. Saturday night at Mario's. The kids in school won't believe it."

"Whoah!" Phoebe grabbed her brother by the back of his T-shirt. "I can't go. Really. Please let's order in. You see, Griffin said he'd call. I still don't know about the audition. I hope nothing's happened to him," she said, nervously glancing at the clock.

Woody practically choked on his soda. "He didn't tell you?"

"Tell me? Tell me what?" Phoebe looked from Woody to Kim, who had picked up the phone and was dialing the pizza shop.

"The big news!" Woody announced dramatically.

Phoebe knew instantly from Woody's face that nothing was wrong with Griffin. She started laughing. "Webster! Stop it. I can't stand the suspense. What happened?"

Kim hung up the phone, and shooed Shawn ahead of her out the front door. "Woody, stop being such a tease." She snapped his suspenders as she walked by. "We saw him, this afternoon at the theater. He was really great. Woody can tell you the whole story. Shawn and I are going to pick up the pizza. They won't deliver this far out unless we order more than two pies."

"You were at the auditorium? You and Kim?" Phoebe was shocked. Of course it made sense. Woody spent lots of time hanging around the Arena Stage. After all, his mom ran the place. Still, she felt vaguely cheated. If Woody and Kim could watch Griffin audition, she should have been there, too.

"Oh, Pheeb," Woody enthused, jumping out of the rocking chair and pacing the room as he talked. "He was great — superlative — the very, very best. Top stuff that guy's got. And to think I, Woody Webster, discovered him. The top star of stage and screen gave his first major performance in Woody's Follies. But he was even better today. He sure learned a lot in New York. I wish you had been there."

"Me, too," Phoebe said sadly.

Woody cocked his head and looked at Phoebe. "Yeah, I know. When I asked Griffin where you were, he said you had planned on coming but he talked you out of it." Woody sat down next to Phoebe on the couch and slung his arm around her. "Pheeberooni, don't look so glum. He figured you understood why he didn't want you around."

Phoebe stared down at the floor. Talking to Woody about her feelings for Griffin made her feel slightly disloyal. Still, she went on, "I did understand last night. I mean, I do. Oh, I don't know." She looked up at Woody, her eyes glistening with tears. "I know what he said. But if it were you, you'd want me with you. I'd want all my good friends around for support, if they could be there."

"But he's not me. He's not you. He's different from almost everyone we know and hang out with. And that's why you love him."

Phoebe hugged Woody. It was good to be with him, especially now that he and Kim were going together. Woody's old romantic feelings toward Phoebe weren't getting in the way of their friendship anymore. And Woody Webster seemed to understand her better than anyone she knew. "Woody, as usual, you're right. So what happened? Is he really going to get that part?"

Woody shook his head ruefully. "No."

"No?" Phoebe wailed.

"He's too young. The director said that he just wasn't professional enough for the Arena Stage productions. And he was probably right. Everyone there was out of college already and had some professional stage credits behind them."

"So that's it!" Phoebe declared. "He didn't call because he didn't get the role. Just like back in New York. Remember, I told you about that!"

Deep down inside she had been afraid of this, that he'd flub the audition somehow and not call her — a repeat of what had happened last year. He had been so sure, just as he had last night, that he'd get a part in a Broadway production. He had actually planned for her to visit him last fall in the city, and then didn't call her, just because he never landed an acting job. Phoebe had gone crazy waiting for him to phone, wondering what had happened. When they finally talked, she knew something was wrong; but he wouldn't admit it at the time. He gave her all sorts of feeble reasons not to make the trip to New York: her parents, his need to concentrate on his work, etc. None of it made sense coming from the impulsive Griffin, and Phoebe suspected he had found another girl friend. But it took ages to find out the truth. He had been too embarrassed and let down to admit that his dreams of stardom on the Broadway stage had come to nothing.

The trouble was Phoebe knew if she had been with him she could have helped him feel better about himself. Or at least if he had talked to her about his problems, she could have encouraged him. She believed in Griffin. As Woody had said once, he positively oozed talent. And in her whole life she had never seen anyone so alive, so full of energy. He would be a star someday, Phoebe was sure of that. When things are tough you want to be — you need to be — with the person you love. What had Laurie said earlier today? "Stand by your man." All Phoebe wanted to do last winter was stand by Griffin Neill.

Chris had told her Griffin's distancing act all had to do with his being so far away. But now he was home, and he was pulling the same number. Phoebe hugged her knees to her chest, and stared miserably into space. She felt useless and empty.

"Earth to Pheeb!" Woody reached over and tousled her hair. "Hey, he might not have gotten the part in Arena's *A Streetcar Named Desire,* but something wonderful happened."

"It did?" Phoebe looked questioningly at Woody.

"Something truly unbelievable. The same director, Bob Jacobs, runs the Maryville Regional Theatre, you know, just west of Carolton. It's geared to smaller productions using young apprentice actors and technicians. He's in the middle of casting *West Side Story*. One look at Griffin, and he practically promised him the role of Tony. Griffin's probably out there now. The casting call was for tonight."

"Outrageous!" Phoebe shrieked, and jumped up. "This is too much. Too, too much. What a break. Oh, Woody, he'd be wonderful as Tony. And the score is so great. I think we have the album with the original Broadway cast somewhere." Phoebe shoved aside the stack of magazines and newspapers that had accumulated in front of the record cabinet and began pulling out albums. She found *West Side Story* and put it on the turntable.

The first side of the record had almost finished playing when the door burst open. "So you told her! I can tell," Kim's cheery voice said from behind them.

"You're back. At last. I thought I would die. I'm starving." Woody greedily eyed the huge box of pizza Shawn was carrying into the kitchen. He slung his arm around Kim's shoulder and gave her a kiss. "I missed you. I thought you'd suddenly gotten a thing for younger men."

Shawn put the pizza down on the table and opened the box. "What younger men?" he piped up innocently from the kitchen door, already reaching for a slice of steaming pizza.

"Let's bring it downstairs and listen to some music. I might even have the sheet music for the piano." Phoebe smiled.

"I'm just surprised Griffin didn't call you himself to tell you the big news," Kim remarked as they descended the stairs.

"Probably all tied up in the reading. The audition wasn't over until six, and Maryville's quite a drive from D.C.," Woody said.

Phoebe just nodded. For the moment, she wanted to savor the sweet feeling of Griffin's success. Thinking of him playing a lead role made her so happy, she wasn't going to let herself worry about why he hadn't called. At least not yet.

Chapter
5

Phoebe's arms were elbow-deep in Woolite when she heard the car door slam.

She had woken up that morning determined to take Grandma Kelleher's advice. She certainly hadn't bothered to last night. Grandma Kelleher used to say, "Never go to sleep on your anger, or it grows hard as a rock and as difficult to move." She also used to say, "Nothing cures depression like dirty dishes, a sinkful of suds, and two hands scrubbing them." Of course, Grandma never had a dishwasher. So hand washing all her own spring and summer sweaters and tops would have to do the trick for Phoebe.

After Woody and Kim had left last night, Phoebe had drifted into her bedroom still singing the refrain to "I Feel Pretty." Only when she had hung her overalls on the big, blue plastic hook outside her closet door did she begin to feel funny inside. The next part of the song kind of stuck in her throat. She glanced at the old brass alarm clock. It was past midnight. Griffin still hadn't bothered to call. Any other guy would have felt midnight was too late. But Griffin wasn't like other guys. He forgot that the rest of the world had schedules and alarm clocks and parents. He used to call her from New York at all hours.

Just as she had flicked out the light, her parents had pulled into the driveway. Any other night she would have run out to the door, then sat with them in the kitchen over cocoa listening to them talk about the concert, and getting her mom to hum softly some of the highlights of the program. But last night, when her mother's low musical laugh drifted in from the front hall, Phoebe pulled the blanket over her head and pretended she was already asleep.

She didn't want to talk to them about music or anything. The only person she wanted to talk to was Griffin. And at that moment she hadn't been sure she wanted to talk to him. The funny feeling inside had turned to anger. It was mean, and inconsiderate, and rude to promise her she'd be the first to know, whatever happened. That was what he had said; those were his exact words when they were sitting together in Sasha's garden.

She didn't remember falling asleep. She only remembered starting to cry, pulling her old yellow teddy bear from the windowsill, and hugging him tight. She lay there feeling angry and hurt and, for some strange reason, frightened.

When she woke up, she still felt all hard and angry, and hurt inside. Now, halfway through her hand wash, she still had the blues.

At first when she looked out the kitchen window, she didn't realize the car had pulled in front of her house and not a neighbor's. It was a red car she didn't recognize, driven by a girl with gloriously long, jet black hair. At least her parents hadn't come back to retrieve something from the garage. They had left an hour ago for their mountain cabin, Sunday being a great day for a drive, and to start planting the summer garden.

Phoebe had just pulled the stopper in the sink when she saw Griffin. He walked from behind the oak tree, looking back at the car and waving at the girl as she made a U-turn. Phoebe's first thought was Griffin, Griffin's here. All her anger, hurt, and hard feelings melted away. He had turned up. At last.

She grabbed a towel and was just about to run into the yard, when the big sunny smile on her face faded. Who was that girl? What was Griffin doing with her? Suddenly the fear she felt last night began to take form.

A second later Griffin burst through the door. "Oh, Phoebe! Phoebe!" he cried delightedly. He tossed aside his small black backpack and threw his arms around her. "Wait until you hear my news!"

Phoebe slipped out of his arms and walked back to the sink without meeting his eyes. "I heard already," she said, busily turning on the water and tossing in her oversized blue-striped cotton T-shirt and a capful of detergent. She kept her eyes on the suds as she spoke. "Woody dropped by last night. With Kim. He told me all about the audition, and how you've landed a part

45

in *West Side Story* out at the Maryville Regional Theatre. That's the news, isn't it?" Phoebe surprised herself. She had never sounded so cold before.

"Woody? Woody Webster told you? That creep. Wait till I get my hands on him. I wanted to surprise you." Griffin fumed. For a second he looked at Phoebe. She had her back turned to him. "Pheeb. Is something wrong?" Griffin said softly. "I mean, you sound so weird. I thought you'd be excited. It's a pretty big thing, not the Arena Stage, but. . . ."

Phoebe bit her lip and stared determinedly out the window. A fat robin was hopping across the driveway. It was a perfect spring Sunday. Several houses down, a lawn mower whirred noisily. Phoebe shrugged her shoulders. Was anything wrong? She took a deep breath. "No," she muttered, then repeated loud and clear, "No. Nothing's wrong. What gives you that idea?"

Then Griffin's hand was on her shoulder. "Phoebe, I just got my first real professional acting job, and you're about as thrilled as an iceberg. Did something happen?" Griffin handed her a towel and turned the faucet off. He made her turn around.

Phoebe kept her eyes focused on the kitchen floor. She willed herself not to cry. When she looked up at him she was dry-eyed, but her expression was cold, hard, and accusing. Phoebe felt as though she were wearing a mask that was too tight. "Phoebe! You *are* really upset. What did I do?" Griffin stepped back. He looked so genuinely confused, suddenly Phoebe couldn't stand it anymore.

"Griffin, you promised. You promised you'd call, no matter what happened. That's what you said Friday night. So I didn't come to the audition. And you didn't call. I waited — " For a second, Phoebe suspected you didn't tell a guy, even a guy you were going with that, but she couldn't help it. "I even tried to call you. And this morning you drive up with another girl. Just like that!" Phoebe snapped her fingers. "And you ask me what's wrong?" Suddenly, she was aware tears were running down her cheeks. She didn't bother to wipe them away. She knew she looked awful when she cried, but she didn't care. All she cared about was that the guy she loved and trusted had let her down.

"Wait a minute!" Griffin exclaimed. "I don't believe this. You mean you thought I didn't call you because I was with Sarah? That's the girl who's the lead in *West Side Story*. She's an actress. I just met her. She gave the whole pile of us a ride back — "

"Back?" Phoebe rubbed her face against her shirt sleeve. "Back from where?" she asked suspiciously.

"Oh, Phoebe!" Griffin took her in his arms. She didn't hug him back. "Phoebe, I love you. Don't you believe that? We were stuck there all night; the whole cast was — at Bob Jacobs's house. The reading went on past midnight. A couple of us didn't have cars, so Sarah offered to drive us back on her way into Georgetown."

Phoebe searched Griffin's blue eyes a second.

She could tell he wasn't lying. "Oh, Griffin, I'm sorry. I just didn't know what to think. I mean — " She twisted and untwisted the towel in her hands. She looked down at the limp piece of striped cotton, and giggled slightly as she tossed it on the counter. "Look at me. I'm such a mess." With one hand she tentatively touched Griffin's arm. "I just got worried, that's all. And I so wanted to know how you did."

"As I said the other night, you're the one who gets dramatic." Griffin smiled and bent to kiss her. A few seconds later he pulled her out the back door, and they sat down together on the concrete steps. Although it was a warm May day, the concrete was still cold and damp against Phoebe's bare thighs. Doing all her hand wash at once had reduced her to wearing a pair of baggy shorts and her short-sleeved Boy Scout shirt.

Griffin cleared his throat and toyed with Phoebe's green plastic earrings as he spoke. "I guess I'm not used to being worried about, Pheeb. It's flattering but — please try not to worry about me. Not that way. The whole time in New York there was no other girl but you."

"I know that, Griffin," Phoebe said softly.

"It's just that I need space. Lots of space. I'm used to it, I guess. Being an actor I don't know what's going to happen next. Like one minute I'm in D.C., next minute I'm fifty miles away, no way to get to a phone. I wanted to call you. But — "

Phoebe put her finger on Griffin's lips. "Yeah. One thing kind of leads on to another, and time flies, and all that."

"You don't sound totally convinced."

Phoebe smiled. Griffin sounded serious, but his blue eyes were twinkling again. "I'm convinced. I'm convinced." She threw up her hands in mock surrender. "It's just that I'm not used to having you around. I thought we'd see more of each other. Now with rehearsals starting right away . . ." she said lightly, but her eyes started misting over as her voice trailed off.

"But we will, we are. Right now!"

Phoebe nodded slowly. They had seen more of each other since he had come back, that was true. She sighed softly. She had hoped they'd be together like Ted and Chris, or Brad and Brenda, or the other couples in her crowd. But Griffin didn't even go to school anymore. It looked as though the Hall and Neill duo would be a couple with a different set of rules than everyone else. She wasn't sure what they were yet, but holding hands at lunch in the quad wasn't one of them. And she didn't know how she felt about that: partly let down, partly free, and very grown-up.

"In fact — " Griffin jumped up and stretched his arms to the sky. He crouched down beside her again and gently traced the outline of her face with his finger. He looked half serious, half teasing. " — seeing each other more is exactly why I'm here. Besides hanging out together and the prom — that's in two weeks, right?" Phoebe nodded. "You're going to help me rehearse."

"I can come to rehearsals?" Phoebe clapped delightedly. She loved the idea of seeing the workings of a real theater.

Griffin shook his head. "I don't know about

that yet, I'll have to ask. Probably not for a while. We don't rehearse the whole thing all at once. I rehearse with the people I do scenes with first, then there are production numbers and dance routines to learn. It's going to be crazy." He ran his hand nervously through his silky brown hair. "So don't set your heart on it," he warned sternly, then winked.

"No, sir." Phoebe sprang up at attention and gave him a brisk salute. "Whatever you say, *sir!*" she barked.

"But I was wondering if you could help me rehearse the songs. You know better than anyone that singing is *not* my strongest point. And it sure is yours. Do you have a piano?"

"Of course, right downstairs. I even have the music out." Phoebe laughed at the surprised look on Griffin's face. "You know the Boy Scout motto" — she pointed to an insignia on her shirt — " *'Be prepared.'* Actually, Woody, Kim, and I were fooling around with the score last night."

"So it's a deal? You'll help me rehearse? I figure if I come over after school during the week, we can get a lot done."

"Oh, I'd love it. I really would." Phoebe smiled, delighted to be able to help him at last.

"In fact, let's get going."

"Now?" Phoebe remembered the unrinsed hand wash stacked by the sink.

"Now!" Griffin said firmly and pulled her by the hand into the house. As he clattered down the stairs in front of her, Phoebe watched him. Yes, Griffin was a great actor. Everything he felt showed all over his body. When he was happy as he was now, even his arms and his elbows looked happy — the whole way he carried himself looked joyful. As Brenda said, with a guy like Griffin she'd never have to worry about him doing crazy things behind her back. He was so up front. Phoebe resolved then and there never to doubt him again.

Janie loved Sunday mornings. Everyone in the Barstow household slept late, except her. Since she was a little girl she had loved waking up early, listening to the first birds, and enjoying the day when it was new. When she first came to Rose Hill she would use this time to be alone, away from the pressures of family and not fitting into the new community. Mornings she'd creep downstairs and curl up on the old, battered couch and read her stash of science fiction and fantasy books.

Today as she tiptoed through the basement workshop, she was careful not to spill the steaming cup of tea she held in her hand.

She looked fondly around her hideaway. But it wasn't a hideaway anymore. It looked more like a design studio. Two dress forms flanked a long cutting table. A second, large commercial sewing machine had joined her mother's old Singer. A gray, metal clothes rack stood in the corner. It was half full of Henry's sample dresses, each one carefully zipped into a plastic garment bag. Thanks to advice from Janie's banker father, Henry's thriving design business had entered a new phase. He was collecting orders for next fall from various boutiques in Georgetown, Philadel-

51

phia, and Baltimore. Meanwhile, he had to cut back on making clothes for the girls at school.

Janie felt sad about that, especially because no matter how busy he was Henry always managed to whip up some fabulous new outfit for her. Her closet was already bursting with great stuff to take her through spring and summer. Still, she was secretly pleased that at the prom she'd be the only girl wearing a Braverman original.

She carried her tea and Danish over to her favorite corner of the basement. Janie had finally reorganized her book niche, and her dad had built a desk for her amid the battery of new white bookshelves. Here Janie often did her homework while Henry worked. But when she was alone she tried her hand at writing. With Sasha's encouragement she began trying at first to write stories like her favorite books: science fiction tales, or fairy tales for her ten-year-old twin sisters.

Lately she had taken a stab at fashion writing. It had all started with a paper for Mr. Barclay's English class. The assignment was to write a review of something from the popular culture. Her favorite TV show was *Star Trek*. But she couldn't figure out what to write about, until Sasha mentioned how weird the women's clothes and hairdos were in *Star Trek*. Suddenly Janie recalled how some of her favorite sci-fi writers were really into exotic fashions for their alien, especially women alien, characters.

So one Sunday she had whipped up a crazy paper on high tech fashion throughout the episodes of *Star Trek*. Not only had she had fun doing the paper, she got an A+, and an invitation to have it published in the school literary magazine. And that had turned into a chance to write a fashion column for *The Red and the Gold*, with Henry as consultant!

Janie smiled as she settled down in front of her stack of yellow legal-sized pads. Her dad had brought a whole new bunch back from the office. Writing on them made her feel so grown-up and organized. She loved them.

She looked down at the sheet in front of her and frowned. It wasn't blank, on it were some measurements. They made no sense. Then a quick sketch. It looked like the dress Henry had sold to Rezato a couple of weeks ago, the yellow one. Had Henry been down here since Friday?

Janie sat back and sipped her tea thoughtfully. Why? Then a sly grin spread across her finely chiseled face. She nodded. Her dress, her prom dress. He was probably working on it here and was going to surprise her.

She only resisted the temptation to snoop for one second, probably half a second. Henry had never told her not to look at his stuff, there was no need to. They usually worked together, and sometimes even Janie's mom helped, along with a sophomore who was a whiz at home ec. Still, he had been strangely mysterious about her dress. He hadn't told her anything about what it would look like. The prom was only two weeks away, and he was very busy with his elaborate plans for decorating the gym.

She tiptoed around the basement, checking first one bin of fabric, then the next. Finally she found some scraps in the wastepaper basket. Red?

Bright red? She tried to recall what Henry had made recently from red silk.

Not a thing. Janie sat down heavily on the bench in front of the old Singer. Sure enough, red thread was on the machine. And yesterday there had been the white stuff he used for his muslin mock-ups.

She stared forlornly at the fabric in her hand. Not that it wasn't beautiful, but it was the one color she really didn't like. Worse yet, she looked horrible in very bright colors, especially red. And with her hair streaked this way, it would really look all wrong.

Then she understood the sketch on her yellow pad, the same dress he had sold to Rezato. It was a nice dress, and he had made it to fit her, like all his dresses. But it wasn't quite her idea of what to wear to a prom, and in red it would look awful on her. Didn't Henry know that?

She bit her lip and felt terribly guilty. Poor Henry, he had been working so hard, he had no time to think up something new. She closed her eyes and thought about what she should do next. Maybe later she'd talk to Sasha; she could trust her not to tell any of the other girls. Maybe together they could figure out some way to tell Henry she had found out about the dress and that it just wasn't right for her.

Then Janie realized something: If he had cut out the fabric already, it couldn't be returned.

Chapter 6

"Caught you red-handed!" a friendly voice shouted, as Phoebe pushed through the double glass doors of the cafeteria.

She looked up as she finished stuffing a couple of sandwiches into her book bag. Woody was grinning at her, and beside him Ted Mason was balancing a heavily loaded tray with one hand. With the other he was already downing the first of two containers of milk.

"Aren't you coming over to listen in to Peter's big announcement?" Ted gestured with the empty milk carton across the lawn toward the crowd's favorite corner of the quad.

"Not carrying two baloney sandwiches, she's not. Not the week before the prom. What would all the other girls say who are on a diet?" Woody asked, in a falsetto. He waved a scolding finger in her smiling face and switched into a gruff-voiced impersonation of Mr. Beman, the principal. "I knew it all along. All the symptoms of a problem teen. Phoebe Hall is a closet sandwich-aholic."

Phoebe giggled. "No, Woody. Baloney-aholic. That's why I love you. You're so full of baloney."

"*Touché!*" Ted laughed heartily, as he led the way down the gravel path.

"I'll join you guys later. In spite of what Woody thinks, I'm not slinking off to a private pig-out. I'm just doing my good deed for the day," Phoebe declared, with a mock martyred expression on her face. "Janie and Henry have been skipping lunch for a week now. Sasha said they're in pretty dire straits trying to get stuff together for the prom. I'm dropping off emergency rations at the theater," she said, a worried look fleetingly crossing her face. Janie had seemed all washed out and limp in Barclay's English class today. Phoebe hadn't seen her looking so out of it since before she started going with Henry last winter.

"They still haven't gotten enough help?" Ted looked concerned. "I'll talk to some of the guys later. And Chris should be able to drum up support at the student council meeting this afternoon."

"After Peter's big noontime scoop, people will beat down the doors to volunteer," Woody predicted. "Sasha's been acting pretty mysterious about his announcement of prom queen candidates. Obviously, she's been sworn to secrecy, but since the ballots appear tomorrow in the paper, she's got to know who's been nominated already."

"Everyone knows who the candidates will be,"

Ted said nonchalantly. But Phoebe smiled at the note of pride in his voice. Whatever secret Sasha had been keeping, it didn't have to do with Chris. For the past two weeks everyone in the junior class had been talking about how the student body president and head of the honor society was about to make history in Kennedy High by taking the triple crown — over all the senior girls, too. Phoebe was delighted her best friend seemed a shoo-in for prom queen.

Phoebe waved good-bye to the guys and hurried across the sun-drenched quad. The lunch crowd was out in full force. Over the weekend everyone's wardrobe seemed to have bloomed into a bouquet of bright spring colors — like flowers. She smiled at the thought. Whistling the song she and Griffin had practiced after school yesterday, Phoebe started up the steps of the old colonial chapel, which now served as the Kennedy High theater. When she opened the heavy oak door, a blast of damp, slightly musty air hit her in the face.

"Janie? Henry?" she called into the dimly lit auditorium. No one answered. Then she spied a yellow wedge of light seeping from beneath the backdrop. They were probably backstage in the prop room.

She leaped onto the stage and pulled aside the stiff canvas curtain. After the dark of the theater, the backstage light was glaring. She blinked a couple of times until her eyes adjusted. Then she blinked again. The cheery "Hi folks!" died on her lips.

Henry was standing on a rickety-looking scaffold, painting the top of a silvery Eiffel tower on a large white sheet. Most of the sheet was already covered with a romantic Paris street scene. He was looking down at Janie, a bewildered expression on his face. The usually fastidious Henry seemed oblivious of the fact that his paint brush was dripping silver puddles all over a bright Folies Bergeres poster lying on the floor.

"Why do you have to paint the geraniums red? That's so corny," declared Janie, stamping her foot and pointing at some freshly painted geraniums to the left of the Eiffel Tower. Her usually sweet face was contorted with anger. Her cheeks were red and blotchy.

"Janie, geraniums *are* red. Paris is full of them. So are the umbrellas. Look. Look at the poster," Henry said patiently. Then he glanced down. "Oh, no! I don't believe this!" he cried, leaping off the low scaffold. He shook his head ruefully as he regarded the silver-blotched poster.

"Now, look what you made me do!" he exclaimed angrily.

"So it's my fault! Everything's my fault around here. You can take your dumb prom and decorations and paintings and drop dead for all I care." With that, Janie burst into tears and rushed into the hall, past an embarrassed and startled Phoebe. A second later a door slammed shut.

"Girls!" Henry growled, then he spotted Phoebe still standing, one hand on the backdrop, the other at her throat. He blushed, and nervously tugged his unruly blond hair.

"Sorry," Phoebe mumbled apologetically. "I

just brought your lunch. I wanted to see if you needed help." She quickly yanked the two sandwiches out of her bag and lay them on a clean spot on the work table. Then she gave an embarrassed wave and scooted back onto the stage, and out of the theater. She stood on the steps a minute looking confused. She felt like she had walked into the rehearsal of a scene from *Ryan's Hope*.

Maybe she should try to find Janie. She probably had run into the bathroom near the dressing rooms. Phoebe debated with herself a minute, then shook her head. Janie hadn't even noticed she was there. She would probably die of embarrassment if she knew Phoebe had witnessed the fight — whatever it was all about. It was hard to believe sweet-tempered Janie blowing up about Henry painting red geraniums in the window boxes of the Paris bistro.

Back at the quad, waiting with the other kids for Peter's broadcast, Phoebe realized that the whole thing reminded her of something. When she remembered what, she giggled. *Alice in Wonderland*, and the Red Queen and the painted white roses. Janie as the ranting Red Queen was such a ridiculous picture. But the giggle was short-lived. She suddenly felt very sad. Couples like Henry and Janie seemed to be really made for each other. They were probably the kindest, nicest, least selfish people she had ever met. Phoebe had always imagined them to be exempt from the kind of problems she had had with Brad. Or from scenes like the one Sunday between her and Griffin. Not that that had been a scene, really. Still, Phoebe had been pretty hurt and angry.

Phoebe's heart caught in her throat as she remembered the hurt look on Griffin's face when she accused him of deserting her for Sarah Carter. "I'm so dumb," she said aloud.

"Talking to herself now!" Woody shook his head and pulled Phoebe down next to him on the bench. He slung one arm around her. His other was already around Kim.

"Well, whoever she's talking to," Laurie said sharply, glancing at her new red Swatch, "she'd better shut up. Peter's coming on right now."

Phoebe blushed. What was Laurie doing here? Then she remembered: Of course, it was a foregone conclusion, in Laurie's head at least, that she'd be one of the nominees. And, Phoebe thought, glancing over at the dark-haired beauty, she was probably right.

"Hey, Cardinals! Isn't Tina Turner something else? She'd get my vote any day. And you'll get more hot Tina tunes in a couple of secs. Today's WKND's special Lucky Ladies Day — Women's Day, for you feminists out there. A whole hour devoted to the best by Madonna, Cyndi Lauper, Bananarama, and of course, Tina. Coming up shortly. After the following announcement . . ."

Phoebe couldn't believe her ears. A hush seemed to settle across the whole quad. Peter's fast-paced rap blared from every radio. Practically the only other sound was the crack of a bat hitting a ball far across the lawn in the baseball field.

". . . by my A-number-one assistant and program manager, Monica Ford. I don't know about you kids out there, but the suspense is killing me."

Laurie moaned. "He's known since Friday!"

"Haven't you?" Brenda spoke up suddenly.

"Of course not!" Laurie snapped. "Only Sasha knows. And she's being a perfect tomb about it all."

Sasha looked up from her bean sprout and avocado sandwich and started to protest. Then Monica's strong, friendly voice came over the airwaves.

"All right, folks. Before I announce the nominees for prom queen, remember you'll get your ballots in this week's issue of *The Red and the Gold*, due out tomorrow. So get out there and vote. And now for the news you've all been waiting for: this year's candidates for prom queen. In reverse alphabetical order; senior, Megan Ranson; senior, Nancy Peretti; sophomore, Mary Lou Lobinowski; senior, Arlene Ferris; junior, Laurie Bennington; junior, Janie Barstow; and last but not least, junior, Chris Austin — "

"Janie Barstow!" Laurie screeched, drowning out the rest of Monica's announcement. "Who's crazy idea was that?! Who would ever vote for Janie — except Henry!"

Chris's blue eyes seemed to grow even bluer. A familiar, determined expression settled over her fine features. "Maybe I will. Lots of people will." Chris got up, and efficiently began collecting people's garbage, tossing the plates and plastic forks into a trash can. She stopped, and planted her hands firmly on her slim hips. "I don't believe you, Laurie. Janie's been looking great this year. Some people just blossom later than others. But maybe you've been too involved with yourself to notice."

Phoebe took a deep breath. She wasn't in the mood to see two people squared off like this for a fight. Laurie was really so tactless sometimes. Still, Chris shouldn't be lecturing her.

"Whoa! Two of our favorite prom queen nominees mustn't come to blows." Ted laughed good-naturedly and put a restraining hand on Chris's arm. "Chris, don't be so hard on Laurie. And Laurie, you know, Chris has a point, too. A lot of kids will vote for Janie. I think it's great she got nominated, though naturally, my vote's already taken. But I have to admit there are lots of other great-looking girls around that I'd have thought of first."

"You bet!" Dick Westergard declared diplomatically, putting his arm around Laurie. "Kim, Phoebe, Sasha, Brenda. But Janie looks wonderful, and lots of people have noticed. There's even a rumor that someone from a modeling agency saw her pictures in Henry's portfolio and was interested in her."

Laurie gave her boyfriend a surprised look. How had she missed that bit of news? Then she promptly dismissed it. Janie a model? Dick was probably exaggerating, as usual.

Then Sasha spoke up quietly, pushing her shiny hair out of her face. "Everyone can't be nominated. But Janie's so busy in that theater painting those props for the prom, I bet she doesn't even know. I don't think the show gets broadcast in there. I'm going to tell her now." Sasha started for the Little Theater.

"Sasha — " Phoebe started to warn Sasha about Janie and Henry's fight. A quick glance at Laurie silenced her. Janie would hate having her problems with Henry broadcast around the school, she thought quickly. "I forgot to tell you, Janie said she needed to talk to you, alone. I think she was backstage somewhere, something about that article." Sasha would be the best person to comfort Janie. Maybe she could figure out what was really going on.

Laurie moodily kicked some mud off the bottom of her good yellow boots. Finally, she looked up and smiled an embarrassed smile. "Chris, maybe you're right. As for Janie . . . well, she'll feel good about it. I can't help being surprised, though." She paused a minute, then added in a puzzled tone, "I know Megan, Angela, Nancy, and Arlene, but who is Mary Lou Lobinowski?"

"Hey, what kind of gossip columnist are you?" Woody shook his head disapprovingly, then hooked his fingers in his suspenders and leaned back on the bench. He sighed dramatically and started, "Mary Lou, sweet Mary Lou. She's — " But before he could say more, Brenda surprised everyone and announced quietly, "She's the new president of the photography club. Only elected last week. I really like her."

"What does she look like?" Ted asked, mischievously watching for Chris's reaction. She smiled coolly. "You've already promised to vote for me."

Phoebe tuned out the rest of the conversation. Whoever Mary Lou was, a sophomore would never be elected prom queen. If they didn't elect a senior, Chris would be the eventual winner. Laurie didn't stand a chance, in Phoebe's book. Too many kids had been hurt by her over the course of the year. And lots of people were still scared of her. Still, she had really gotten her act together lately. And so many of the guys around Kennedy practically fainted whenever she walked by. . . . Megan was too cute. And Angela had lots of spirit and beautiful eyes, but she looked more like a pom-pom girl than a prom queen.

But Janie? In a crazy way Janie was turning out to be more beautiful than Chris or Laurie, or anyone Phoebe had ever seen. She shifted uncomfortably on the bench, and glanced at Chris out of the corner of her eye. Had she actually been thinking of not voting for her best friend? Chris was the one who seemed to have everything, and Janie. . . . Laurie had been right: It would make Janie feel so good.

Chapter
7

Phoebe stared skeptically at the beaker of frothy purple liquid.

"Wasn't this supposed to turn pink?"

Peter Lacey shoved his Walkman down over the collar of his lab coat. "Pink, blue, purple — something like that!" He tapped his pencil rhythmically against his notebook and glanced quickly up at the clock. Still moving to the beat of music only he could hear, he whispered hoarsely, "All right! Just five more minutes, Pheebie-jeebie. Let's start cleaning up."

Phoebe readily nodded agreement. Chemistry must have been invented to torture people who hated being neat, precise, organized, analyzed, and labeled — that is, most of the kids Phoebe knew. The only good thing about chemistry this semester had been Peter switching lab sections and ending up as her partner. All the other girls in the class drooled with envy. Not because Peter was any help at unraveling the mysteries of science — he hated chemistry as much as Phoebe and barely managed C's — but because the fast-talking, handsome DJ had been voted the most desirable guy at Kennedy. And, until recently, the one least likely to fall in love.

Phoebe hadn't cared about any of that, though Peter sure was great to look at. But after a long-distance romance with Phoebe's old friend, figure skater Lisa Chang, Peter had fallen for someone closer to home, his new station assistant, Monica Ford. In any event, cute as Peter was, he wasn't Griffin. He was just a friend, and lots of fun to be in class with. He was also the only person Phoebe knew, beside herself, who had gone through all the crazy changes that loving someone far away involved.

Peter gave a disgusted snort and bravely dumped the smelly purple liquid into the sink. Phoebe stifled a laugh as Ms. Barish walked by.

"Purple?" The teacher shook her head despairingly. "You two will have to repeat that experiment next week," she said sharply and walked away, her high heels clicking her disapproval.

"Wonder what color we'll get next time?" Phoebe whispered, just as the bell rang.

Peter chuckled and flashed Phoebe his famous grin. "Three o'clock, at last. Talking in a whisper's going to ruin my resonant radio voice. So how's Griffin doing? Did he get the part he was talking about the other night?"

As she wriggled out of her lab coat she explained about Griffin landing the role at the Maryville Regional Theatre. "I've been helping

66

him rehearse the songs. He's doing great. You wouldn't believe how wonderful he's sounding since taking all those lessons in New York."

"Yes, I would. And he wasn't half the singer you were to begin with," Peter commented, holding the door of the science building open for Phoebe. "In fact, speaking of *your* singing: How's it going? I got lots of great feedback from that live bit you did for us. A couple of other kids want to try their luck behind the mike."

"Maybe Woody could arrange something for your show, a live broadcast mini-Follies."

"Featuring Phoebe Hall!" Peter said. "How about it, Pheeb. Let's try another gig on the air."

Phoebe kicked at some twigs on the ground. "I don't know, Peter. I guess I thought it went all right when I sang for you, but now. . . ." Her voice trailed off. She remembered what Griffin had said after the broadcast. "Not bad for a beginner." He had pretended he was kidding, but his blunt criticism had not only hurt, it had made her think. Sure, she had a good voice. Singing was what she loved to do best. But there were so many talented people out there and most probably sang better than she did. She didn't feel like making a fool of herself again.

"Hey, don't look so blue about it. Didn't you listen to that tape? It was far out, Pheeb. You've got the right stuff."

"Griffin doesn't think so," Phoebe blurted out, then wished she had kept her mouth shut. It sounded so — she wasn't sure what. Dumb? Or it made it sound like Griffin was jealous. He wasn't, she knew that. He had only been trying to keep her from getting her hopes up. He had suffered a lot of hard knocks in New York himself. She'd be really stupid not to listen to him.

"Well, he's nuts. Tell him Peter Lacey knows a thing or two about music and singing." Peter stopped on the edge of the parking lot and glanced down at Phoebe. His sparkling green eyes looked very intense and serious.

Phoebe smiled in spite of herself. Peter's charm was irresistible. Besides, something in her wanted to believe she really could be a singer if she tried. Anyway, what else had Griffin said? "He didn't say I couldn't sing, Peter. Really he didn't. He just said stuff about lessons and training, and all of that. I had thought it was something I more or less could do naturally, you know?"

"Want to talk about this some more at the sub shop? I promised to meet Monica there. Sasha might have some advance copies of the paper by now."

"I'd love to. Speaking of singing, I've got to go to chorus. Thanks for the encouragement. And I'll mention the idea of a broadcast Follies to Woody, if that's okay."

"Pheeb, you know I'd love it! And you'd better be the star of it." Peter settled his Walkman over his ears, half closed his eyes, and danced his way across the parking lot to his metallic-gold Volkswagen.

"Phoebe Hall, you're an idiot!" Phoebe muttered aloud and slammed her locker door shut, giving a quick spin to the combination lock. One leg of her sweat pants was sticking out of the bottom of the locker, but she didn't notice. She rushed down the empty hall. One of the problems being five-foot-two was being stuck in the front row of the chorus. Squeaking in late was going to be tricky business.

Phoebe wasn't feeling stupid about being late, she was feeling stupid about being Phoebe. She had watched Peter dance his way toward his car and had been struck by how happy he looked. Music was his passion, and being a DJ was exactly what he wanted to be doing. And he was lucky enough — no, Phoebe corrected herself — *directed* enough, to be doing it.

Last fall Phoebe had felt pent up, frustrated, and held back by being Brad's girl friend, and not being whatever it was she wanted to be. Now with Griffin, it was the same. And yet, it wasn't the same at all. That confused her, because she and Griffin had similar dreams. She was helping him with his dream of being an actor, and she loved it. Rehearsing with him the past few days had been heaven. After they'd say good-bye, the love songs they had sung together at the old rickety basement piano would stay in her head all night. Loving music had gotten all mixed up somehow with loving Griffin.

But all at once, halfway to the sprawling main building, it occurred to Phoebe that helping Griffin sing wasn't doing much to make her own dream come true. She wanted to be on stage. Phoebe wasn't sure what kind of singer she wanted to be. She only knew she wanted to be a great one. One tape didn't prove a thing, not when you were only sixteen. And talking to Peter suddenly made her realize that if she only could figure out how, she might have a chance at a singing career. But if she didn't try she'd never be completely happy, even with Griffin back in her life.

As she turned the corner leading to the auditorium, Phoebe skidded to a halt. A sad, haunting melody was coming from the music room. Phoebe felt herself drawn toward it like bits of iron to one of Shawn's toy magnets. It would only take a minute to peek inside and check out what record was playing. She paused a moment, her hand on the doorknob, a smile of recognition crossing her face. She *had* heard something similar before, when her mom and she had gone to a classical song concert in the Folger Shakespeare library last winter: a woman's deep alto voice accompanied by a single cello.

A shiver went down Phoebe's spine. Quietly, almost reverently, she turned the doorknob and peeked inside the cluttered room. She managed to stifle a gasp. There was no record; only a lanky, dark-haired boy playing a gleaming cello, and beside him, a tall, slender black girl singing the words; eyes closed, her face full of emotion.

She had seen the girl around before, with a senior guy from the debating team. She was extremely beautiful, and Phoebe wondered for a second why she wasn't in chorus. She leaned against the doorframe, her chin lifted up, and let the music envelop her like the fragrant breeze on a summer night. Suddenly, it ended.

"Oh!" she cried, clapping her hands. "I've

never heard anything so beautiful. Never, in my whole life. What was it?"

The cellist spun around in his chair. The startled look on his thin, handsome face gave way to the warmest, biggest smile Phoebe had ever seen. The girl sank into a deep curtsy, and managed to look gracious in spite of her tight jeans. With a throaty laugh she stuck out her hand.

"Hi, I'm Wanda Davis. This is Michael, Michael Rifkin. And the composer was John Jacob Niles. He's great, isn't he?" Her voice was deep and musical, somehow giving Phoebe the impression she was still singing as she spoke.

Phoebe quickly shook hands, then introduced herself. She had never heard of John Jacob Niles, but she made a mental note to look him up in the library.

"Phoebe Hall! That's right." Michael carefully rested his cello against the wall and unfolded himself from the chair. Phoebe figured he was taller than Griffin by at least three inches. "I remember you. You sang that great solo from the *Messiah* in the Christmas concert." Turning to Wanda, his dark brown eyes shone with excitement. "Remember, I told you? The junior with that really clear soprano voice."

"Right, Michael. *I* remember. And I quote, 'The really pretty redhead.'" She eyed Phoebe approvingly. For a second Michael looked embarrassed.

Phoebe felt a blush come on. It was one thing for Griffin to say she was pretty, but it felt sort of weird coming from a guy she'd never even seen before. Weird, but nice. She studied her

71

sneakers for a moment. When she looked up, Michael was busily tucking his cello into the big, black carrying case.

"Who do you study with?" Wanda asked, gathering together music from a music stand.

"Study?" Phoebe repeated, puzzled.

"Your singing teacher," Michael explained, leaning back against the crook of the old grand piano. He seemed so confident and sure of himself as he stood there. For a second Phoebe envied him. Like Peter, or Griffin, he had that happy look of a person who knew exactly where he wanted to be going, and was well on his way to getting there. Then she realized he was expecting her to answer a question.

"My singing teacher?" Phoebe shrugged, then giggled. "I've never studied singing. I had a year of piano lessons — when I was eight." Suddenly she felt so unaccomplished, and silly. After hearing Wanda's voice, how could she imagine herself having a career singing. And Wanda was probably only a year or so older than she.

"Well, you should, from what Michael tells me," Wanda said firmly, grabbing a stylish gray cotton jacket off the back of a chair. "And don't let that smile fool you, he's very very critical about music. Try my teacher. She'd love you. I've got to run. Michael can give you the address. See you tomorrow, Rifkin."

With that, she was out the door. "I don't know." Phoebe hesitated as she watched Michael scribble a name and number on a piece of looseleaf paper.

"But I do. You really have talent. At least give

it a try. Phone and make an appointment for an audition — " Michael broke off and winced as if in acute pain. Before Phoebe could ask what hurt him, she heard for herself.

Down the hall the first strains of "If Ever I Would Leave You" floated out of the auditorium. The music sounded tinny; all the sopranos were singing flat. Chorus rehearsal had started.

"Oh God, I'm late!" Phoebe ran out the door. She turned and waved at Michael, who called down the hall after her. "Think about it, at least." Phoebe grinned good-bye, then skidded into the auditorium.

Mr. Leopold was tapping his baton on the podium. He glared at Phoebe as she slipped into position in the front row. Sally Newholt pointed out the place in the music. Phoebe glanced down; in her hand was the crumpled piece of paper. She unfolded it slowly. Michael's writing was bold, open, and very messy. But the name of the teacher sounded like a beautiful song — Rosa Spinelli. That clinched it. Wait until she told Griffin tonight. She was going to take a real risk. She was going to call Wanda's teacher right after school and make an appointment for an audition.

"Phoebe Hall, being late is nothing to smile about. Wipe that grin off your face and SING." Mr. Leopold tapped his baton angrily and the music started up again. Phoebe pasted on a serious expression. But inside she wore a smile wider than Michael Rifkin's.

73

Chapter
8

Janie sank low in the passenger seat of Sasha's Rabbit. She twiddled the wide strap of her hobo bag and stared gloomily at her knees.

It was certainly one of the most miserable days of her life. She was almost convinced that she had been better off before meeting Henry Braverman and getting all mixed up in this clothes business, and caring so much about how she looked. This morning her deepest fear about her dress had been confirmed. Looking for her slipper under the basement couch, she found a mysterious, large, white box. Inside, carefully wrapped in tissue, was a brilliant red silk dress, the same design as Henry's yellow one inside Rezato. Sometime between Saturday and Tuesday he had whipped it up — just like Henry. He had hidden it, hoping to surprise her for the prom. Janie promptly burst into tears. She felt so awful. There was no way she could look good in that dress.

She knew she had to talk to someone, so she had called Sasha. The two of them had been riding around for about an hour, trying to figure out what to do. Sasha pulled over to the curb and turned off the ignition. As she turned to face Janie, her huge brown eyes were full of concern. "I still think the best course would have been to tell Henry exactly how you felt."

"Sasha Jenkins, tell the truth. If you were me could you walk up to him and tell him the dress he spent all that money on making for you — and all that time — is all wrong, and you can't bring yourself to wear it?" Janie challenged.

Sasha bit her lip and studied her hands. "To be honest, I'm not sure. Still, it's what I think I should do, I mean if I were you."

When Sasha had trotted into the ladies room to tell her she had been nominated as a candidate for prom queen, Janie thought it had been some sort of cruel joke. Except Sasha never joked, not that way. Sasha had been pretty shocked when Janie burst into a renewed bout of tears and sputtered how she wouldn't be going to the prom. Besides, the whole idea of her even being nominated was totally ridiculous. But it had felt good to finally confide in somebody, anybody, about the fiasco with Henry and the red dress. She hadn't meant to yell at him about geraniums, she had just wanted him to get the point. She didn't like red. But unlike guys in the romances she had read, Henry couldn't take a subtle hint. And it had all blown up into a stupid fight.

It was a warm spring afternoon, but Janie

suddenly shivered. What if he stayed angry with her? What if they never talked again? Sasha said that calling him tonight should make everything okay. After all, Sasha and her boyfriend Wesley always had lots of fights. Making up was actually fun. Sasha had giggled when she said that.

Janie wasn't convinced. Making up after a fight with someone you loved couldn't possibly be fun. At the moment she felt too embarrassed to ever face Henry again. Over the phone — maybe she could try to apologize that way. But Janie had always hated talking to people on the phone; you couldn't see their faces.

Sasha started the car again, and she and Janie rode in silence to the Barstows' house. The car halted in front of the white, rambling two-story house, and Janie got out. "Think about what I said," Sasha urged, before she drove off.

"Janie, where have you been?" Mrs. Barstow called from the pantry. "Henry was over here looking for you. Then he called a couple of times. I thought you were staying late at school because of the prom."

Janie hung up her jacket and hurried to the basement stairs before her mother could see her face. Her mother always knew when she was lying. "Oh, I had an errand to run with Sasha. You know, for the paper. My interview for the prom is in the next issue, all that stuff."

As she clattered down the stairs, her mother called, "Well, don't get too involved down there. Dinner's almost ready."

"Don't worry, Mom." Janie quickly pulled out the red dress again. She held it up to herself in front of the mirror. Well, maybe it wasn't her dream prom dress, but if she didn't wear it she knew Henry would be confused, surprised, and maybe a little hurt. On the other hand, maybe Sasha was right: She should be honest with him.

Janie had just finished repacking the dress and sliding the large white box under the couch, when she heard a footstep on the stairs. She quickly sat down and opened a book lying on the sofa. It had to be one of her sisters or her dad.

"Janie?" Henry's voice was soft and hesitant. She looked up, a mixture of guilt, fear, and relief on her face. He was standing at the foot of the stairs, his head nearly level with the exposed, thick beams of the old colonial house. In one hand he held a bunch of bright white daisies.

"I've been looking for you all afternoon." His long, nervous fingers ruffled his hair. "Are you okay?" He sounded so vulnerable and scared, Janie thought her heart would break.

"Oh, Henry." Janie jumped up, and threw herself in his arms. "I'm sorry. I really am. I didn't mean to be such an idiot." Suddenly the whole scene with Henry in the theater seemed so dumb and unnecessary. "I can explain everything. Really, I can." Before she could say anything more, Henry's lips found hers. The flowers dropped from his hands onto the couch.

A minute later he was whispering in her ear. "There's nothing to explain. I love you. People have fights. Anyway, I changed the geraniums to pink. They look prettier that way."

"But Henry," Janie pulled back a few steps. "It really had nothing to do with geraniums. I was upset about — I have to tell you — I found the dress you made for me."

"You did? I mean, that's impossible."

"And — and that's why I got so upset about the red geraniums, because I didn't think I would look good in a red dress."

"Red dress? Janie, what do you mean?"

As Janie pulled out the big box again and opened it up to show him, Henry hit his head with the palm of his hand and sank down onto the couch. "Oh, no. You found Laurie's dress."

"*Laurie*'s dress?" Janie looked confused and slightly hurt. "You made a dress for Laurie? But I thought I was the only one you were going to make a dress for. You said — "

Now Henry was holding his head in his hands. "Oh, Janie, try to understand. I was only going to make a dress for you, but I couldn't afford to buy the material that I needed. Then Laurie came along and offered to pay me for that dress. So I did it . . . for you."

Janie folded up the dress and put it away. "Now I won't be the only girl at the prom in a Braverman original."

Henry pulled her down beside him on the couch. "Yes, you will. Laurie's dress is just a copy of the one I made for Rezato. But your dress will be one of a kind." He silenced her protests with a passionate kiss. Janie wound her arms around him, and for a single dizzy moment she felt it wouldn't even matter if she wore her pajamas to the prom.

Chapter
9

Brenda Austin reached for the blue willoware pitcher and poured herself another glass of milk. She had more or less lost track of the dinner conversation. She had been thinking of Brad, and the feeling in his voice when he had said he loved her just now, on the phone.

He'd be coming over after dinner to drive her to her weekly meeting at Garfield House, the halfway house Brenda had gotten involved with last fall. Actually, it was "their" weekly meeting now; Brad had gotten interested in the troubled kids who found shelter at Garfield. Tony said Brad had the makings of a really good counselor. Brenda secretly hoped he'd steer his medical career toward psychiatry. He was so very good with people.

A faint smile played across her hauntingly lovely face as she sat back in her chair and debated taking another piece of homemade chocolate cake. She had already put a generous slice aside in the kitchen, to take to Brad for lunch tomorrow. As she reached for the cake dish, Chris's words, drifting toward her end of the formal dining room table, didn't quite register — not at first. Brenda glanced up quickly at her sister. Was she still talking about Janie's nomination for prom queen?

"Who is this Barstow girl, anyway?" Chris's father inquired, beginning to sound a bit bored with all this talk about a dance.

"You know, the daughter of the banker who moved here from Cincinnati last year," Mrs. Austin reminded him gently. "I hear she's quite bright and has started up a successful dress design business with that boy Henry Braverman. They sell his clothes at Rezato."

"And Janie's really turned out great," Chris enthused, her blue eyes all sparkly and bright. "It took a while for her to fit in. But now — well, kids who have been around Kennedy for years didn't get the nomination. You know, like Phoebe or Sasha. . . . Not that they minded, though," she added quickly.

Brenda leaned her elbows on the lace tablecloth and peered intensely at her stepsister. Why was Chris going on and on like that? Mrs. Austin cleared her throat and glanced in her daughter's direction. Brenda quickly took her elbows off the table and balled up the linen napkin in her hand.

"I've got to get ready. Brad's coming any minute now," she murmured quickly. She pushed back her chair and began clearing the dishes. As she pushed through the swinging doors leading to the spacious, modern kitchen, she glanced over her shoulder at Chris. Chris's laugh sounded forced, Brenda thought. And since when did the confident but usually self-effacing Chris Austin hold forth for an entire hour about proms, homecoming, and getting elected student body president? What was she trying to prove?

"You *are* upset!" Brad Davidson looked across the passenger seat toward Brenda. She was fairly tall, but she looked small, diminished somehow, by the way she sat, her thin arms wrapped around her chest, her knees drawn up beneath her. She was staring out into the soft rain.

"No, not really. Not upset. I'm just thinking," Brenda replied. A hint of a frown crossed her face.

Brad reached across the seat. Gently, he massaged the back of her neck. The muscles were all hard, tense. She closed her eyes and leaned into Brad's soothing hand.

She kept her eyes closed as she spoke. "I can't figure it out. Chris is not acting herself. It's got something to do with the prom. . . ."

For a second the only sound was the slap of the windshield wipers. Then as Brad pulled into the driveway beside Garfield House, he said cautiously, "Are you sure it's Chris that's bothering you? Last week you weren't even sure *you* wanted to go to the prom."

Brenda's eyes popped open. "Oh, Brad. We settled that. I do want to go — with you. As long as I don't have to buy one of those goofy dresses.

I would feel so weird, walking around like something from a Miss America pageant." She stuffed her hands into the pockets of her old jean jacket, and faced him with a shy smile. She studied his square-jawed face. She unbuckled her seatbelt and slid next to him. With her finger she traced the outline of his strong, handsome features. A year ago, whoever would have thought she'd find such a steady guy and fall in love. Crazy runaway Brenda Austin dating a Princeton-bound senior. And happy for the first time in her life. "Oh, Brad," she exclaimed as she took his hand between both of hers, "I'm not at all worried about me and the prom, or me and you, or anything like that. Things are perfect right now. But something's definitely bothering Chris."

"She looked okay to me, this afternoon in the sub shop." Brad pulled the key out of the ignition. "Though she has a way of doing that."

"Doing what?"

"Looking great, no matter what's going on. Phoebe always used to say that Chris can put on a good front. If it hadn't been for Laurie blabbing it to the world last year, I doubt anyone would have known about her breakup with Ted."

Brenda absently nodded agreement. But tonight she hadn't looked great, or actually, she had looked too great. Too perfect. Too happy. Too *on*.

"Brenda, I can tell you already have some kind of theory; out with it," Brad challenged with a smile.

Brenda colored slightly. Outside of her friend Tony at Garfield House, Brad was the only person she had ever met who could read her mind; sometimes it was downright embarrassing. "Okay. I think Chris is upset about Janie being nominated for prom queen." As soon as she said it she wished she could have taken the words back. After all, she had no proof. It was all just a hunch.

"*What?*" Brad gasped, then burst out laughing. "Chris wouldn't feel like that. In fact, Ted told me, he was quite proud of the fact, too, that Chris announced her intention of voting for Janie."

"That's what I mean." Brenda looked directly at Brad. "I guess I shouldn't sound so sure about this. It's probably not even true. But what's that line from Shakespeare I learned last week? 'The lady doth protest too much!' You've known Chris for ages: She's always been elected head of everything, including homecoming princess. When did she ever make such a fuss?"

"Chris Austin always makes a fuss." Brad chuckled, but the laugh died quickly on his face. "Except it's usually about other people." The popular future student-body president was known for always championing the underdog on campus, even her own stepsister. But Janie surely wasn't an underdog, not anymore.

"Forget I mentioned it," Brenda said suddenly, reaching for her pocketbook. She didn't like it when Chris talked to her friends about her, and she was beginning to feel disloyal confiding her suspicions about her sister to Brad.

Brad started to say something, but one glance at Brenda's face silenced him. Apparently the

Austins' most notable trait, their fierce determination, could be acquired by adoption. Brad decided to bide his time and have a talk with Ted later.

As they hurried across the lawn and up the broad steps leading to the halfway house, Brad teased, "So tell me. Who *are* you going to vote for for prom queen?"

Brenda paused thoughtfully. "I'll vote for Chris. I'd feel disloyal otherwise. Though, really, I wanted to vote for my friend from photography club, Mary Lou."

"She's pretty — looks like a tamed-down version of Phoebe," Brad said, a wistful note creeping into his voice.

Brenda had learned over the past few months not to be too jealous. After all, Brad had dated Phoebe Hall for two years. It was only natural he should miss her sometimes. Still, she was glad when Brad put his arm around her shoulder and gave her a quick kiss.

"And who's your pick?" Brenda laughed a throaty laugh. "Laurie Bennington, I bet."

"Bennington!" Brad roared. "No way."

"Come off it, Davidson," Brenda protested. "Aren't you the one who says every kid deserves not just a second but a third, fourth, and fifth chance to straighten out?"

"Okay. You're right. She has gotten better, I guess." He sounded dubious. "But still — by no stretch of the imagination is she my idea of prom queen. The only guy in our crowd voting for her is Dick Westergard. As they say, love is blind — to a lot of things."

"You still haven't answered," Brenda teased, as they walked in the door. Voices drifted out of a large room down the brightly postered hall. At least the meeting hadn't started yet.

"I thought about it. You know, I think I'm going to vote for Janie. Chris is the head of so much stuff. And somehow . . . when I went out with Janie that one time, to homecoming, I got to thinking she's one of the sweetest people I've ever met."

Just then Tony poked his head out of his office door. "About time, you guys. It's a really good group tonight." He strode over toward them, hugged Brenda, and put his arm around Brad's shoulder. "So how are my two favorite people these days!"

Brenda let Brad do the talking. Her mind was spinning. She wouldn't tell Brad for all the world, not now. But she knew for certain what Chris was afraid of. If Laurie was the only real competition, the prom queen crown would go to Chris hands down. But with sweet and very attractive Janie Barstow suddenly in the picture. . . .

Brenda's heart began to ache for her sister. For the first time in Chris's charmed life at Kennedy High, she was faced with the possibility of losing an election. And the golden girl had never had to learn how to deal with losing.

Chapter
10

Phoebe sat cross-legged on her bed, twirling the frayed ears of her furry rabbit slippers. In just twenty hours and ten minutes she'd see Griffin again. Just twenty hours and ten minutes before she could watch his face when she told him her big news. She knew exactly how his eyes would light up and crinkle around the edges. He'd be so happy for her. How was she ever going to stand the waiting?

"Okay, your turn, Pheeb. In which two plays does Marc Antony appear?" Chris asked crisply, tapping the end of a well-sharpened pencil on the white painted surface of Phoebe's cluttered desk.

No answer. Chris peered over the edge of her Kennedy High loose-leaf notebook. Her blue eyes narrowed to a critical squint. "Phoebe Hall, you aren't paying attention." She repeated the question, sounding very much like the spectacled schoolmarm in *Little House on the Prairie*, Phoebe thought. She shoved a stray red curl out of her eyes and guiltily consulted the large hardbound book on her lap.

"*Romeo and Juliet*. That's one!" she said promptly.

Kim slapped the floor with her hand and practically choked on a piece of sushi. "I don't believe you!" She laughed heartily, reaching for the green bottle of Perrier. "Wake up, Phoebe. Remember earth? Come down from orbit. We finished *Romeo and Juliet* three questions ago."

"Oh," Phoebe said meekly. Chris and Kim had come over after dinner to help her cram for tomorrow's English test. But it was so hard to concentrate on anything, especially plots of Shakespearean plays. Her head was so full of music. Ever since she had called Rosa Spinelli this afternoon, she'd been mentally going over every song she knew.

Even on the phone, she loved the singing teacher's voice. She had a faint Italian accent, and her laugh sounded like a bunch of little, tinkling bells. Phoebe couldn't quite picture her, except she knew instantly she wouldn't be very old, even if she *was* a famous teacher. She also knew instantly she'd love her. With all her heart she hoped she'd get through the audition and be accepted as a student. Of course, then came the hardest part: convincing her parents to cough up all the money for lessons. But she'd cross that bridge Friday afternoon.

"I'll give you a hint," Chris continued relentlessly. "One of the plays has his name in it."

"Whose?" Phoebe looked genuinely puzzled.

"Marc Antony's." Kim quickly came to her rescue. "You know, like blank and Cleopatra."

"*Antony and Cleopatra!*" Phoebe finally exclaimed, slapping her forehead with her hand. "But what else? I just don't remember. I'm sorry."

Chris took a deep breath. Phoebe could see Chris was on the verge of a really fierce mood. But that wasn't Phoebe's fault, there had been so little time for homework the past couple of weeks. First there had been all the extra choral practices, and now Griffin was back, and all those after-school rehearsals with him. As Griffin said once, you had to live your life according to what was important to your dreams. Making her dreams come true had nothing to do with learning Shakespeare.

"*Julius Caesar*. You know, Antony's the guy who gives that great speech," Chris explained testily. " 'Friends, Romans, countrymen, lend me your ears.' Really, Phoebe, for someone who wants a stage career, you really had better do something with your memory. Actresses have to be quick studies."

"I only can memorize stuff when there's music to it, like songs. I never forget a song once I've heard it. You know that," Phoebe mumbled truthfully, feeling a little hurt. Sometimes Chris sounded like such a know-it-all.

She flopped down on the blue quilt and stared across the cozy room at the old oak dresser. She had picked some wild flowers from down by the river. They were yellow and purple and white, and would dry really nicely. She had tucked them in the frame of Griffin's picture — a new one, a real professional headshot from a New York studio.

"I give up!" Chris threw her hands up in the air. She stood up and stretched, then adjusted her off-white sweater over her trim gray slacks. "Let's take a break, at any rate."

"You bet!" Kim said, bounding to her feet. "Anyone want some sushi? I made lots. It's my favorite study food. Fish is supposed to be good for your brains."

Chris glanced skeptically at the neatly rolled rounds of raw fish and rice. "I've never tried it."

"Mmmm," Phoebe moaned. "Looks great, I am starved. But I'm on a diet."

"Hardly any calories. Lots of protein."

"Stop it, Kim. You're beginning to sound like Sasha. If you tell me it's that healthy, I'll lose my appetite fast." Phoebe picked out a piece and bit it. "Yummy."

"So, is everyone ready for the prom?" Kim asked, bouncing over to touch her toes, then doing some side stretches. "I think it's cruel to have any tests the week before the prom — bad for the figure. Bad for the head, too." Kim flicked on the red plastic radio on the bureau. She began moving in rhythm to the new Julian Lennon tune.

"We got our dresses Saturday," Chris said. "Phoebe's is really outrageous."

Kim's round, cheerful face beamed with expectation as she kept dancing. "Can I see?"

"Do you really want to?" Phoebe asked shyly. Kim nodded vigorously. "I'll try it on. It's in my mom's closet."

Chris raised her eyebrows. Phoebe laughed and dropped her voice to a whisper. "They kind of blew up at the price, but when I put it on my mom actually liked it. I'm just committed to lawn mowing all summer, and weeding the garden up at the cabin." She slouched dramatically against the door frame, then scooted across the back hall to her parents' room.

"Out-of-sight!" Kim screeched as Phoebe stepped back into the room, still adjusting the strap of her dress. "Where did you ever find it? And look at those shoes!"

Phoebe was still narrating the crazy story of her foray with Brenda down to a Georgetown thrift shop for antique tap dancing shoes, when the phone rang.

"It's for you, Phoebe," Mrs. Hall called from the living room.

"Oh, it's Griffin!" Phoebe clapped her hands and ran into her parents' room. She closed the door behind her, and picked up the phone.

"I've got it, Mom!" she said and waited for the kitchen receiver to click down.

"It's me," Griffin said.

"How are you? How was the rehearsal today? Sorry I had to skip our duet bit. Chorus is pretty hectic these days. I just can't miss a practice." All the words tumbled out of Phoebe's mouth all at once. She had so very much she wanted to tell him.

"Oh, Phoebe, rehearsals get better and better.

90

You've got to come sometime. In a week or so. I checked with Bob Jacobs. He said once the production numbers are worked out we can ask guests. Do you think you can make it?"

"Can I make it?" Phoebe snorted. "Who are you kidding? I'd even skip chorus." She giggled. "Though I can't be responsible for what Mr. Leopold might do when I finally did turn up."

"But I really missed being with you today." Griffin's voice deepened slightly as he spoke. "I was trying to sing 'Maria,' but I kept feeling inside I was singing Phoebe."

Phoebe blushed and stared down at the shiny shoes with the crazy grosgrain-ribboned bows. She knew exactly how he felt. It had only been one day since they'd last seen each other, but she felt as though a part of her was missing.

"Phoebe?" Griffin's voice sounded hesitant. "You all right?"

"Of course. I'm fine. I'm perfect. I'm wonderful. But you'll never guess why."

His laughter filled the phone. She could picture him now: head thrown back, a hint of color in his clear complexion, his eyes all twinkling and bright. If they were together now, his hand would be on her shoulder or her face, and she would want to start kissing him and never stop. "If you tell me someone else is making you this happy, I'll just die." But from the way he said it, Phoebe knew that he knew better than anyone there'd never be someone she'd love this much again.

"Boy, I heard actors get pretty big egos — " Phoebe scolded playfully. "Maybe it's not you

I'm happy about at all." She swayed back and forth as she talked, toying with the taffeta flounces on her skirt.

"Oh!" Griffin pretended jealousy.

"Actually, I don't mean to be secretive." Phoebe sighed, looking at the clock. After all, Chris and Kim had given up their evening to study with her. "I just want to surprise you. You'll have to wait till tomorrow. It's such incredible news, Griffin. I want to tell you in person."

"Oh, Phoebe." All the sparkle abruptly went out of his voice. "I can't see you tomorrow."

"But why?" Phoebe's heart seemed to catch in her throat. She stood still, cupping the phone close to her ear.

"You know all my stuff is still in New York. Well, I got a ride. A couple of the kids from the theater offered to help me; one of them has a van. We'll leave right after rehearsals tonight. Then I can be back by Friday evening — in time for Saturday's schedule at the Regional."

"Oh, Griffin!" Phoebe sank down on her mother's bed. She couldn't think of what to say. She had really looked forward to being with him tomorrow. Still, she reminded herself bravely, he had told her last weekend his schedule was bound to be crazy sometimes. Like it or not, if loving Griffin was part of her life, she'd have to get used to his breaking dates. "Well, my secret will keep." Even as she said it, the smile returned to Phoebe's face. By Friday night she'd *know* for sure if she was taking lessons. If the audition worked out, the news would be even more exciting.

"But listen, Pheeb." Griffin lowered his voice. "Your parents can't hear me, can they?"

"No. Of course not."

"Come with me, Phoebe. Please. You can cut classes. It's only a couple of days till the end of the semester. I so want to be with you." The way he said that made Phoebe's heart stop.

"No, Griffin, I can't. I can't do that," she finally managed, her voice trembling. "I have a test tomorrow. And my last trip up to the city didn't go over too big, especially when my folks found out from Woody's mom about everything that happened." Then she remembered the Friday audition. "Even if there weren't all that — I just can't. It has to do with my surprise," she added quickly.

Phoebe could feel Griffin's disappointment over the phone. For a second he didn't respond. Then he cleared his throat. "Okay, I'll be back Friday. I'll see you then. But I'll miss you, you know that."

"I know." Phoebe closed her eyes and smiled a soft, tender smile. "Me, too," she added.

"I love you," Griffin said.

"I love you." Phoebe quietly hung up the phone. It was such a beautiful way to say good-bye. "I love you," she whispered to the empty room, then quickly scrambled out of her dress and back into her painter's pants.

"It's so great," Kim said a few minutes later, finishing off the last bit of sushi, "that he can take the time off from rehearsals to take you to the prom."

"I never thought of *that*." Phoebe suddenly

93

panicked. "I never even asked him about it. I mean, we talked about the prom before he got the job. Oh, Chris, what will I do if he can't make it?"

"Now don't get all freaked out," Chris soothed. "Griffin's coming to your prom. He would have told you if he couldn't make it."

"Sure." Kim shoved her blunt cut hair off her face. "Anyway, rehearsals don't last all night, proms do."

Phoebe stared at the floor a second then looked up shyly. "I guess you're right. He would tell me, wouldn't he? I mean, if there had to be some crazy kind of change. Like he did just now."

"It's sad he has to go to New York, but it's only one day," Chris reminded her.

Phoebe debated with herself for only a second. "It's not just that. It's not just being away for one day. It's — Listen, you two. . . ." She beckoned the two girls closer. "Can you really keep a secret?"

Chris gave her a hurt look. "How can you ask?"

"I knew it!" Kim grinned wickedly. "All night you looked as though you were about to explode like a basket full of firecrackers. What's up, Hall? Out with it. And I promise I'll never breathe a word."

"I haven't told anyone yet." She got up and paced over toward the window. The rain had stopped. The lilac leaves were shiny in the light streaming from the house. When she turned around, she was smiling. "I'm going to do it. I'm going to take singing lessons."

"You are?" Both girls shrieked in unison.

"Shut up!" Phoebe glowered. "I haven't told *them* yet." She nodded toward the living room.

"But lessons are really expensive, Phoebe. You can't pay for them yourself," Chris whispered.

"Of course not." Phoebe explained her plan. "Then after the audition, if it goes well — "

"*If!*" Kim exclaimed. "Phoebe, you know it's going to go well. It has to, you were made to sing. When you were a baby you probably sang for your bottle, instead of crying like us other mere earthlings."

"Oh, Kim," Phoebe scoffed, trying to brush off the compliment. But she didn't really want to; somehow she felt Kim was right.

"But remember," she added quickly, "don't tell anyone. Not Ted. Not Woody. Please. I want Griffin to be the first to know. Even before my parents."

"He's going to love it, Pheeb," Chris said warmly.

Phoebe hugged her old friend and had a strange thought: Something was wrong with Chris. She seemed so tense and preoccupied, but she had been too caught up with her own dreams of Griffin and her Friday audition to really take it in.

For the first time all night Chris looked relaxed, more herself. When she had walked in earlier with Kim, she was chattering away about Janie's nomination. But what bothered Phoebe had been the way she had looked. All wound up, like a blue-eyed, blond-haired doll, with a brightly painted, perfect smile.

Chapter
11

Rosa Spinelli's house was wonderful, even from outside. Phoebe had never seen so many balconies, porches, turrets, and bay windows; every one full of flowering plants. In spite of the rain, several windows were thrown open. The faint strains of a violin drifted out from an upstairs room into the cool spring air. The place looked like something Sasha might have invented when she was into writing ghost stories, back in the seventh grade, except it wasn't a scary house.

But starting up the curved flagstone path toward the front door, Phoebe was definitely scared — scared and delighted.

Her rubber boots squished as she splashed through the puddles and up the wooden steps of the porch. At the door she hung back a moment and closed her eyes. She whispered a silent prayer. She had this crazy feeling that when the door opened she'd be walking into a whole new life and out of her comfortable old one. And in spite of everything she had learned since meeting Griffin about taking risks, new situations still petrified her, especially walking into one alone. Griffin Neill sure had been nuts going to that Arena Stage audition by himself. She would give anything to have him here with her. Of all days for Griffin to be up in New York.

She took a couple of deep breaths and rang the doorbell. No one answered right away. Maybe Miss Spinelli had forgotten all about the audition. She forced herself to ring again and tried to hum a tune, any tune. But every song she had ever known seemed to have vanished from her head. Phoebe panicked; in the next few minutes she was going to have to sing for a complete stranger, and she couldn't remember how. How dumb could she be, imagining she had what it took for a stage career.

Just then, the large white door opened. Phoebe found herself eye to eye with a slim, dark-haired woman with an enormous smile on her finely featured face. The smile was warm, inviting, and oddly familiar.

"You must be Phoebe. Welcome."

Phoebe managed a quick nervous grin and stuck out her hand. Her throat felt dry, and she was sure she couldn't remember how to speak, so she didn't try to say anything. She leaned against the wall and pulled off her red boots. She hung up her slicker, next to a child-sized yellow one. Another, even smaller, pink raincoat hung on a low hook. Phoebe had had one just like it when she was six. She loved it so much she wore it every day, rain or shine. On her seventh birthday she had cried because it didn't fit anymore.

Miss Spinelli put her hand on Phoebe's shoulder and guided her into an enormous lace-curtained room off the front porch. "Wow!" Phoebe suddenly found her voice and gaped at the black concert grand piano in the corner.

"Make yourself comfortable. I'll bring us some tea. Honey and lemon is great for the throat on a day like this. Isn't it?"

"Uh, sure," Phoebe mumbled as the small energetic woman hurried off down the hall.

By the time Phoebe finished her tea she felt perfectly at home. She felt as though she had known Miss Spinelli her whole life. The teacher wasn't scary at all, even if she was famous. Phoebe naturally found herself chatting about school, Woody's Follies, Griffin and New York, and her dream of being a singer someday. She had almost forgotten about the audition. She felt as if she were visiting the family of a good friend, like Chris or Sasha. She sat back in the overstuffed chair and sighed a contented little sigh. Someday she'd love to have a room like this: stacks of music, a canary in a cage, and the wonderful smell of something baking in the oven floating in from the hall.

"Well now, maybe we should begin!" Miss Spinelli's voice broke into her daydream. She briskly opened the piano and sat down. Phoebe was still holding her empty teacup. She gulped as the teacher motioned for her to stand up, next to the piano, facing her.

Phoebe's hand shook as she carefully set the

delicate flowered cup and saucer on the coffee table. When she stood up her legs suddenly felt as limp as overcooked noodles. In spite of the soothing tea, her throat had gone all dry again. She had felt something like this when she tried out for Woody's Follies, the first time she sang with Griffin. If only Griffin were here, she thought desperately, I'd get over this. I'd look in his eyes, I'd be able to sing anything in front of anyone in the world.

She stuffed her hands in her overalls pockets and crossed her fingers. Then the first note sounded on the piano.

To Phoebe's amazement she didn't have to sing anything — not exactly. Miss Spinelli would play a single note on the piano and ask Phoebe to sing the note. After the first couple of notes, Phoebe made a game of matching her voice to the sound of the piano. It was easy, like a kid's version of *Name That Tune*. From the expression on Miss Spinelli's face she could tell she was matching the notes very well.

Then she had to sing a couple of scales, just like warm-up for chorus. She never thought she'd be grateful to grouchy Mr. Leopold, but suddenly she was; the scales were a real cinch.

"Now, let's try a song. You mentioned liking show tunes. Let's see what I have here." Miss Spinelli rummaged in an overflowing music cabinet behind the piano. She pulled out a couple of thick, hardbound books. Phoebe eyed them curiously. One was an opera score. The other was *The Messiah*.

"I sang something from this once." Phoebe

pulled *The Messiah* toward her. "Last year, I did a solo in chorus."

"Ah, yes," said the teacher, as if recollecting something.

Phoebe frowned. Had she mentioned *The Messiah* over tea just now? Before she could give it another thought, Miss Spinelli was playing the introduction to Phoebe's old solo. "This is what you sang, isn't it?" Before Phoebe could reply, the teacher was counting the beats of the introduction, and Phoebe found herself singing the familiar melody.

At first she could hardly hear herself. Her voice kind of squeaked out a thin, pale sound. But Miss Spinelli didn't seem to notice, she just kept playing the accompaniment and humming the choral parts. She played so spiritedly that Phoebe gradually forgot all about auditioning and just began singing. Her clear soprano voice soon rang out like a bell. By the finale she had a joyous smile on her face and was swaying with the strong rhythms of the music. When the piano stopped, her heart was still singing.

"Fantastic!" a familiar voice cried. Phoebe whirled around. Michael Rifkin was standing in the doorway, softly applauding, an old striped umbrella tucked under his arm.

By his side stood a goofy-looking little boy, about Shawn's age. He had a solemn expression on his thin, sensitive face and was wearing a pair of green Mr. Spock ears and a *Star Trek III* sweat shirt. "You really are good!" The grave little face lit up in an enormous, wide smile. It matched Michael's perfectly.

Phoebe stammered, "You take lessons here, too?"

Both boys burst out laughing. "From Mom?" Michael said incredulously. "I'd die first!" Michael winked at his mother. "Me, too!" His brother contorted his face, but he obviously hadn't mastered winking yet.

Phoebe burst out laughing and turned back to Miss Spinelli. "You're Michael's mother?" Suddenly the familiar smile made sense. Spinelli must be her stage name or maiden name.

"Yes. And this is my son Paul." She introduced the little boy. "But speaking of lessons, you're going to be late," she warned sternly, handing Paul some music from a stand beside the piano. Paul squirmed into his slicker, stuffed the music into his backpack, picked up an instrument case, and started out the door.

As an afterthought he poked his head back in. "Live long and prosper!" He gave Phoebe Mr. Spock's famous Vulcan salute and clattered down the porch steps into the rain.

Phoebe burst out laughing. "I've got a brother just like that."

Michael grimaced. "You mean there may be two of them?"

"Does he play oboe, too?" Miss Spinelli asked, closing the piano and pushing up the sleeves of her cream-colored knit top.

"Oboe?" Phoebe repeated, puzzled, then grinned. "No. He wants to play the drums, but my father has some objections."

"I can imagine." Michael laughed. "Fortunately the Rifkins are into string instruments, oboes, and voice! Percussion passion hasn't hit this house yet."

"Well, Phoebe, Michael was certainly right about you," Miss Spinelli said, as Phoebe headed for the hall to put on her boots. "I would love to have you as a pupil. You have a very promising voice. And no matter what kind of music you want to sing, even rock 'n' roll, it won't hurt to have the training. But I only take on serious students. You would have to come twice a week."

"Do you mean it?" Phoebe glanced from Miss Spinelli's smiling face to Michael's. "Oh, I'd love it! Twice a week!" Phoebe's eyes shone. "I'll ask my parents tonight. As soon as I get home." She stood a minute, one arm inside her raincoat, grinning like an idiot in the middle of the hall. Could this really be happening to her, Phoebe Hall? She couldn't wait to tell Griffin. Suddenly she had a funny feeling Michael was watching her. She must look pretty weird standing dumbfounded in the middle of his front hall. She quickly scrambled into her coat and reached for her umbrella. Phoebe glanced at her watch; her mother would already be home, wondering where she was. "Gosh, it's late. I'd better go. I don't want to miss the bus."

"The bus?" Michael shook his head in disbelief. "You came all this way on a bus? Come on, I'll drive you home."

"You don't have to do that," Phoebe protested. But she gratefully accepted the offer; even in rush-hour traffic the car would be faster. Besides, she felt so full and happy she didn't want to be alone, not on the day when her most cherished dream was coming true.

"I think I've got it straight!" Phoebe laughed over the music on the radio. "In the Rifkin/Spinelli orchestra, Paul plays the oboe, you play the cello, your little sister plays the violin, and your brother in Rome — the piano? Oh, wait, make a left at the next corner. I live down this block." She scrubbed at the fogged-up van window with her sleeve. Her mother's station wagon was parked in front of the house.

Phoebe felt sad that she was home already. It had been a long drive from Michael's house, but even with traffic delays it hadn't seemed long enough. She was surprised to hear that he loved all sorts of music, not just classical. On the way home they had both sung along with some tunes from the country music station. Then Michael spun the dial and gave a whoop worthy of Peter Lacey when he located a tune by Talking Heads. Michael knew all the words to "Life During Wartime," but Phoebe only joined in for the chorus. Now Michael was half singing along with Springsteen as he filled her in on the details of life with his eccentric musical family.

"Nick plays organ, too," Michael was saying. "You'd really love my dad. He's off in Topeka organizing a choral society. It was really wild at home when Mom was still performing and Maria was still a baby. She mainly teaches now. Though sometimes she's gone for a week to judge competitions."

"This is it. This is my house." Phoebe turned to Michael and smiled. "It's crazy we never met before in school. I know some kids you'd really love. Next time we have a party you have to come." She squeezed his arm and laughed. She was trying to remember when she had last laughed so much. It must have been with Woody. But Michael didn't tell jokes like Woody. He just seemed to enjoy everything so much: the music, the rain, the flock of yellow school buses in the grade school parking lot. Maybe that's why he smiled so much. He seemed to be in love with life. And looking at the world through his eyes made everything seem so alive.

Phoebe sighed happily. She wondered if Michael had a girl friend — Wanda, maybe. She'd have to find out. If not . . . ? Too bad all the girls she knew were already involved with someone. Still, she had other friends. And everyone she knew would really like him, especially Griffin.

He'd love Griffin. Phoebe grinned. She would introduce them. They'd really get along. Maybe she'd throw a party soon, after the prom was over, to celebrate Griffin's opening. "Yes, Michael, I'll do that soon. I'll throw a big party. And you have to come."

"I'd like that," Michael said, tossing his head to get his longish dark hair out of his eyes. "I could bring some of my friends, if it's okay with you. It's hard imagining not having run into you sooner, too. Kennedy's crazy that way. There are so many crowds of people, so many little worlds there, it's amazing. You can be in one world and not know another one even exists for three whole years."

Phoebe knew exactly what Michael meant. She had never even seen Griffin before the auditions for Woody's Follies, but he had been around Kennedy for almost four years then. She couldn't imagine what her life would be like now if their worlds hadn't touched.

"Well, we did meet," Michael was saying. "And I'm glad to find such a great new friend." He tipped an imaginary hat, then reached over to open her door.

Phoebe started laughing again. She jumped out of the van and waved good-bye until the tail-lights vanished around the corner. By the time she got to the kitchen door she remembered when she had laughed like this.

Not with Woody. Not with Griffin either. It had been on the phone, last week sometime, with Chris. She couldn't remember what started them. It never seemed to matter. Ever since junior high when they first became friends, every so often they would look at each other and laugh and laugh and laugh, for no good reason, just for the joy of it.

Yes, Michael Rifkin, Phoebe thought, you're going to be a really good friend.

Chapter 12

Phoebe leaned across the table and fished one of Ted's fries off his plate. She raised her voice and shouted above the din of the jukebox, and the Friday night crowd. "I said, it was really out of sight. You should have seen the house. Mom said I could go twice a week, and they'd pay for the lessons. Even Dad looked happy about it." She had to shout louder and louder as the Iron Maiden record boomed toward its climax. "And you should see the family. There's this crazy kid brother. He's got a bad case of the *Star Trek* syndrome — green ears and all."

"The teacher's brother has green ears?" Ted shouted back across the table, waving one hand in the direction of the door. Phoebe looked around. Brad and Brenda had just walked in.

"No," she continued, "Michael's brother. And wait till you hear what he does. He's only ten."

Phoebe's voice suddenly rang out across the sub shop during a lull in the music.

"Let's hear all about it, Red. Exactly what *does* Michael's brother do?" some wiseguy at the next table called out to Phoebe. She gave him a dirty look and slouched deeper into the corner of the booth. Obviously a conversation at the sub shop was going to be impossible. She had dragged everyone over here in case Griffin came around looking for her. But it was already past nine, and he probably wasn't going to turn up.

"Who's Michael?" asked Chris, glancing up from her diet soda, and making room for Brenda at the end of the booth.

Phoebe glared at her friend. Today was the most important day of her life. Her boyfriend was wandering around somewhere between Rose Hill and New York City, and now her best friend was in a spaced-out mood. "You haven't heard a word I said. I told you three times already."

"Sorry. Guess I'm just a little out of it, Phoebe," Chris apologized. "Tell me again. This time I'll listen, I promise."

Brenda caught Phoebe's eye and gave a sympathetic shrug. Chris had been acting a little weird for days. Everyone was beginning to notice.

Phoebe took a deep breath and said again, "Michael Rifkin, the guy I met playing cello when Wanda Davis was singing. You know her, at least. It's his mom, Rosa Spinelli, who's the teacher."

"I know him," Brenda spoke up softly. You could barely hear her above the music. "He's in

107

my history class. You remember, Brad, the guy I told you about."

Brad laughed. "Right, real handsome and a musician. He sounded so perfect I thought you made him up to make me jealous."

"Oh, stop it." Brenda reached across the table and tugged Brad's hair playfully. "Really, Phoebe, he's a wild guy. Good wild, not bad. He manages to center all his papers on music. Like music during the Civil War, music during the depression era. Mr. Caryle suggested he try music and the cave man next. He was being sarcastic. The next week Michael walked in with a tape of some primitive music from the bush people in Australia, plus what he called original instruments. Gourds, weird bones — stuff like that. The class cracked up, but the music was great."

Phoebe giggled. That was just the kind of thing Michael would do. "That sounds like him. Anyway, his kid brother is so good at the oboe, he just gave a concert at a big hall in New York."

Chris suddenly slapped her hand on the table. "I've got it now. I *do* know him. Rifkin's the guy who sometimes conducts the student orchestra. He's really nice. I met him at a student council meeting last month. He's a little like Lisa Chang: very involved in his music and not much time left over for school activities."

But he wasn't like her skater friend Lisa, Phoebe already knew that somehow. Michael just moved in a different crowd than her own. He had lots of friends. Somehow music made him more sociable; a little like Peter Lacey.

"Hey, here's Romeo!" Ted snapped his fingers in front of Phoebe's nose.

She turned around, startled to see Griffin elbowing his way through the crowd. "He made it!" she whooped and ran toward him.

"Griffin, Griffin, wait until you hear." She threw her arms around him and kissed him, not caring about the whistles going up from a nearby table.

Griffin gave her a quick kiss on the cheek, then smiled a slow, tired smile. "You look so happy, Phoebe."

"Of course I'm happy. You're back, and I've got such good news," she bubbled and pulled him by the hand over to the table. "But you've got to try to guess what." Phoebe waited a second. When he didn't respond, she teased. "Okay, I'll give you a hint. One hint. You gave me some advice up in New York. Remember?"

Griffin shook his head. He pushed back a stray curl that had worked its way out of Phoebe's thick braid. He studied her pretty face for a second, then sat down in the booth and looked down at his hands.

"Hi, Griffin!" Ted whacked Griffin on the back. "Did you hear what Phoebe did when you were off carousing in New York?"

Griffin looked up. The usual hint of color on his high-boned cheeks was gone. He needed a shave, and his hair looked grimy. He glanced quickly at Phoebe. Her face was wreathed in smiles. She sat herself down on his lap and grinned. "I'm going to do it, Griffin, take singing lessons."

109

"Hey, Pheeb, that's great!" Griffin squeezed Phoebe's shoulder and rubbed his hand against her neck. It took a second for the smile to fade from her face. The way he touched her felt like the way Chris looked when she told her the news — not very interested.

She slid off his lap and sat next to him in the booth. She looked up into his face. She'd never seen him look so flat and played out.

"Griffin?" She didn't have to put her question into words. He squeezed her hand.

"Just tired." Phoebe suddenly felt very selfish. She had been so involved in getting through her audition, she hadn't thought about how wiped out Griffin would be from moving.

"So aren't you going to finish telling us about your teacher, Mrs. Rifkin?" Brad asked.

"Miss Spinelli," Phoebe corrected. "She teaches under her maiden name."

"Rosa Spinelli?" Griffin asked, the color returning to his cheeks. "Does she live near Potomac?"

"Yes," Phoebe said. "You've heard of her?"

Griffin straightened up and smiled. "Sure. A lot of kids in the show have studied with her at one time or another. In fact, Sarah — remember Sarah Carter, the girl who plays Maria? — still studies with her."

"Does she like her?" Phoebe asked, shifting uncomfortably in her seat. How could she forget Sarah, with the red car and beautiful dark hair.

"Like her!" Griffin waxed enthusiastic. "She's considered the best teacher in the D.C. area.

110

I'm impressed you're going to study with her. From what Sarah says, Rosa Spinelli changed her whole life."

"Pheeberooni, Griffin — you're back!" Woody shouted from the door.

"Hey, Webster, keep it down to a dull roar!" Tony called from behind the counter.

"How could shiny, wonderful me ever be dull?" A chorus of groans greeted Woody's pun. Laurie and Dick Westergard followed Woody in.

"Honestly, Woody, we can't take you anywhere without you making a scene," Laurie teased in a breathy voice, as Dick and Woody shoved a table up to the crowd's favorite booth.

"Where's Kim?" Brenda asked.

"Don't ask." Woody heaved a dramatic sigh. "The course of true love never does run smooth. How did I ever fall in love with a career woman? Earthly Delights got some last-minute catering job over in Maryville!" he exclaimed, referring to the successful catering business Kim had started with her mom. He buried his dark curly head in his arms and pretended to sob. A second later he popped up again wearing a goofy grin.

"Speaking of Maryville — how's life in the big time, Griffin?" he asked, hooking his thumbs in his suspenders.

"We were just talking about that when you walked up," Griffin said animatedly. "Phoebe's going to be taking singing lessons from the teacher of my leading lady in the show, Sarah Carter."

"Singing lessons?" Woody's eyes grew wide.

"Pheeberooni, it's about time." He leaned down the table and planted a kiss on her cheek. "I'm so proud of you. Tell me all about it."

Phoebe bit her bottom lip and smiled shyly. "I don't know much about it yet. I guess I'll be studying all sorts of stuff . . . even opera, if you can believe that!"

"Opera. You'd better watch it. Opera singers get fat," Laurie warned.

"They do?" Phoebe frowned, then shook her head, remembering beautiful Wanda and Michael's slim, vivacious mother. "Come off it, Laurie. How many opera singers do you know? I've met two, and they're both perfectly normal-looking. Better than normal, actually," she concluded loyally.

"Sarah's not fat," Griffin interjected.

"How are rehearsals coming?" Dick asked, shoving up his glasses on his nose.

"Fabulous. I've never had so much fun in my life. It's hard work, though, and any interruption seems to break your concentration, even stopping to go home for the night."

"Then why'd you go to New York?" Brad asked.

"I had to get my stuff out of the apartment, and a few of us didn't have rehearsal calls yesterday and today. It'll make it hard to get back into the mood tomorrow, though. We did go over lines in the car. Next week we start full cast calls. I can't wait. Sarah and I start stage rehearsals of all our scenes late next week. It's moving so quickly. I still can't believe it's happening." Griffin's eyes shone. He nervously tugged his hair and was fairly bursting with excitement. Talking about the theater always brought him to life, Phoebe thought.

A quick glance around the table brought a proud smile to her face. All eyes were riveted on Griffin. He always automatically became the center of attention, without even trying. It was hard keeping her eyes off him. Talking about theater, he didn't look tired anymore, life and energy burst from every pore. His eyes were all electric and twinkly again. With his scruffy beard and frayed cotton shirt, he looked sort of like Harrison Ford on the set of an adventure movie. All he needed was a red bandana around his neck to complete the effect.

My God, she suddenly thought, someday he might even be a movie star. The thought bothered her somehow, she wasn't sure why. She couldn't exactly picture Hollywood, but it seemed a long way from her world. What was he saying now?

"Sarah told me that last time Bob Jacobs directed a play out at the Regional the production ended up touring the country all the next winter. I'd have work for a year, unless something better turned up."

Phoebe caught her breath sharply. "You may go on tour?"

Griffin nodded enthusiastically. He began talking about the Guthrie Theatre in Minneapolis, and the director of another production of *West Side Story* who might be coming to check out the Maryville opening, mainly to cast Maria. But when he saw Sarah he'd also be seeing Griffin. Who knew what could happen?

Woody and Ted joined in the conversation. Phoebe slouched back in her seat. Griffin's arm was around her as he spoke, but she felt as if he weren't touching her, as if there were this big space growing between them. A big empty space. No, not an empty space, a space filled with one name — Sarah.

She tried to ignore the feeling. It was silly. It was plain green-eyed jealousy, and she knew it. There was nothing between Griffin and Sarah. Hadn't he told her that last Sunday?

"Hey, Chris, you're being pretty quiet." Ted's voice broke into Phoebe's thoughts. She looked up. Chris was struggling into her sweater. Her blue eyes looked very blue and sad. Phoebe wanted to kick herself. She had been so involved in her own excitement about Griffin, and now singing lessons, she still hadn't tried to have a heart-to-heart with Chris.

"Is it time for the movie?" Phoebe asked, reaching past Griffin for her jacket. "The Bogart festival's closing tonight at the mall. *Casablanca*. We were going to head over there . . . unless you don't want to." She paused before slipping it on. "I mean if you're too tired, or whatever."

"Do you want to go?" Griffin asked. His voice sounded flat again. Phoebe felt her heart catch in her throat. A minute ago he had been so alive, and now. . . .

"Do you have to ask?" Woody groaned. "Phoebe's practically made a ritual of sobbing her way through that film. Starting with the credits. I can't believe she hasn't dragged you to it yet. You two have been going together for

114

months —" Woody quickly cut himself off as he caught Phoebe's eye. She looked as though she wanted to kick him under the table. As though she wanted to say, So what if Griffin doesn't know what my favorite movie is?

"Then we'll go," Griffin declared, and led the way out the door, followed by Ted and Chris. Phoebe trailed behind, her hands stuffed in her jacket pockets, fighting back her tears, and having no idea exactly why she felt like crying.

By the time Ingrid Bergman had just asked Sam to play it, one time for her, Phoebe knew exactly why she was crying. It had nothing to do with *Casablanca* or the mournful opening notes of "As Time Goes By." Next to her, Chris was sniffing loudly, her lovely blond head cradled in Ted's shoulder. Ted's hand was caressing her soft, long braids.

But Phoebe and Griffin sat slightly apart, their shoulders barely touching. Griffin stared straight ahead at the screen, as if he had never seen the classic flick before, as if he were trying to memorize every one of Bogart's moves. With her sleeve, Phoebe scrubbed away the silent tears that ran down her face. She tried to see Griffin's expression, but she couldn't, the back of the theater was too dark. She could feel his intensity. Maybe he didn't go to movies and hold hands like normal people. Maybe he really did study the films.

Then Bogie was leaning on the old bar saying, "Of all the gin joints in all the towns in the world she had to walk into mine," and Phoebe let out a loud sob. Griffin instantly had her in his arms.

With one hand he wiped away her tears, as he rocked her gently back and forth. Phoebe didn't even pretend to watch the movie. She let herself cry into the familiar softness of his old cotton shirt.

"Don't cry, Phoebe. Don't cry," he was whispering in her ear.

Chris glanced over. She tugged Ted's arm. "We're going for popcorn." She sniffed and pushed Ted out the other end of the back row.

Griffin's hands smoothed across Phoebe's back in a strong rhythmic movement. She lifted her tear-stained face to his and found his lips in the dark. They clung to each other that way for what seemed like forever. Finally, Griffin broke away and rested his cheek on her head, staring dully at the screen as if he were trying to sort out his thoughts.

Ever since his return to Rose Hill, Griffin had known that something had been different between him and Phoebe. He loved her so much. But last fall everything had felt so free, and impulsive. Now something had changed, things between them had become all complicated, and closed, and held in. Tears started down his own face. Finally he whispered, "I love you so much, Phoebe. So very much. If you had only come with me to New York — " Then he was afraid to say more, so he found Phoebe's mouth and kissed her deeply, holding her as if to keep her from slipping through his hands.

Chapter *13*

Chris Austin looked in the locker room mirror and wanted to scream. If only I could be like Phoebe, she thought. I would scream. Or shout. Or burst into tears.

But she didn't scream. She turned away from the mirror and leaned her back against the cool porcelain sink. She wrapped her arms around her chest and stared forlornly at the white tiled floor. In spite of her thin cotton shirt, she was roasting and freezing at the same time. Which was crazy, because it was the first really warm day of the year and she had just played two sets of tennis with Ted on the school courts, beating him both times.

Winning didn't make her feel any better; she always won. Being a winner was as much a part of her as her blond hair, her straight nose, and her even white teeth. It was probably built into her genes. After all, how many juniors in the history of Kennedy High had been elected student body president? One: Chris Austin. The day of her victory Phoebe had teased her, saying the next step was the White House. Hadn't Chris sworn to be the first woman president of the United States, when she was just eight years old; and failing that, the first woman astronaut? Well, Sally Ride, her idol, had beaten her to outer space, but no woman had made the White House, not yet.

Actually, the idea of being any kind of president made her feel sick at the moment. She deserved to be impeached, at least that's how she looked at it. A flush of color spread up her neck and onto her face. She had actually, for the first time in her life, lied; in a nasty, stupid way. Monday morning when she had turned in her ballot for prom queen, she had said to at least three different people, including Laurie Bennington, that she was voting for Janie.

She had meant to, she really had. But talk had reached her about how even Phoebe was thinking of voting for Janie, and she had gotten scared. She had never lost an election before, and it would be so humiliating not to get the prom queen title.

At the last minute she had grabbed an extra copy of the paper and pulled out a fresh ballot. She stealthily checked her own name, folded the paper in neat squares, and tossed it in one of the ballot boxes near the gym.

A minute later she felt like an absolute traitor. Janie passed by and smiled gratefully at Chris. Obviously, word had reached Janie about Chris's very public statement about her dumb vote.

"I hate you, Chris Austin," she muttered, kicking at the tiles with her sneaker. "I hate you more than anyone in the whole world." Then the first tear fell, and another, and another.

"Chris, there you are!" Phoebe poked her head in the door. "What's wrong?"

"Nothing." Chris quickly splashed some water on her face. "I'm just hot. You know how tough tennis with Ted can be." She reached for her bag.

Phoebe leaned against the door, shaking her head. "You can't fool me. You've been crying, and it sure isn't over losing a tennis match. Come on, out with it. I mean, what are friends for?" Phoebe reached over to give Chris a sympathetic pat.

Chris wrenched away her arm. "Leave me alone. I'm sick of all this. Do you hear? Just because I feel like having one little cry, everyone gets into a panic. You know, Pheeb, I have feelings, too." Suddenly the tears were streaming uncontrollably down her face.

"No one said you didn't," Phoebe replied quietly, feeling a little hurt and confused.

"Well, every time *you* have a cry, the whole world doesn't come barging in to find out what's wrong. Do they?"

Phoebe started to laugh, then stopped. Chris hadn't joined in. This was the point where Chris would usually see how self-righteous she sounded and burst out laughing and crying, and all the tension would evaporate. Then she'd talk about what was really bothering her.

Instead, she splashed some more cold water on

her face, shouldered her bag, and stormed past Phoebe out the door.

"But, Chris," Phoebe called in a small voice. "I really needed to talk to you."

Chris whirled around. Her eyes were flinty; an icy expression had settled on her finely chiseled features. "Sure, you, and Brenda, and Ted, and Brad. I'm sick of it. Why don't you just mind your own business — all of you." With that, she strode down the hall and around the corner, out of sight. A second later the door to the outside banged shut, and the echo reverberated through the empty locker-lined halls.

"But it *was* about my own business," Phoebe said softly to herself as she wandered desolately back into the locker room. She hadn't seen Griffin since Friday night, and she was scared. It was high time she talked to a friend. But Woody was off at the sub shop with Kim, and Sasha was holed up in the journalism room. She felt funny confiding in Brenda. Who knew where she was, anyway?

Just when the one thing she needed most in the world was her oldest best friend, Phoebe felt she didn't have a friend in the world.

Chapter
14

Janie reached into the back of Henry's station wagon and pulled out a heavy carton. She rested, with one knee on the tailgate, and wiped the sweat from her face with the sleeve of her old paint-stained shirt.

She hoped it wouldn't be this hot on prom night. The gym would be suffocating, even with all the doors and windows opened. All the fresh flowers Sasha had insisted should be part of the springtime in Paris theme were going to wilt.

Janie glanced across the quad toward the empty tennis courts, where an hour ago she had seen Chris playing a pretty intense game with Ted. Janie sighed with envy. Here she was, lugging decorations to the gym in her grimy jeans, drowning in a sea of sweat, and Chris had managed to look perfectly cool and competent dashing around the court in the unseasonable heat. Even in her crisp tennis whites she looked to

Janie like the ideal prom queen. Chris would probably wear a classic, floor-length white dress, with a little flower at the waist, to the dance; the kind of thing Janie had always dreamed of wearing herself, but she knew that would make her look all washed out. Janie sighed. She couldn't help wishing, just a little, that somehow she'd end up winning the election. But it was a crazy idea. Even if she were wearing the dress Henry had made for her, she felt that she didn't look at all like a prom queen. That's why she had marked her ballot for Chris.

She hoisted the heavy box out of the wagon and started down the path to the bubble-topped gym.

"Janie, I've brought the troops."

"Oh, Peter. Just in time." She gave him a shy welcoming smile. Her old romantic feelings for Peter had gone up in smoke when she met Henry. Still, ever since homecoming last fall she'd felt embarrassed around the handsome DJ. It was hard looking a gorgeous guy in the eye after he had found out what a terrible crush you'd had on him for a year. She still considered him a friend, and had really been flattered when he had finally taken notice of her as something other than an able assistant. As luck would have it, it was the same day Henry had asked her on their first date. Not once had Janie regretted her decision to choose Henry.

"I promised you new recruits daily, and I'm here to deliver. Come on, guys, get the stuff out of the car. Let's get a move on!" Peter pulled out a couple of cartons and led the helpers into the gym.

Janie grinned. One of the "guys" was Monica. "I insisted Peter stop at the sub shop first," Monica explained. "Here are some Cokes and a couple of sandwiches. Sorry I haven't been able to get around to help sooner. Everything's been so crazy, what with counting the prom queen ballots, and all." Because Laurie Bennington was a nominee, Monica had somehow ended up in charge of the voting committee. Janie quickly looked down at the rolls of pink crepe paper sticking out of the heavy box. She muttered something about lugging it right over to the gym, then half-scampered away, terrified Monica would see from her face that she harbored secret hopes of winning.

Henry poked his head out of the gym and shouted, "Janie, where's that crepe paper?" Then he noticed the parade of volunteers led by Peter Lacey, and his narrow face lit up. "Wow. I've got a regular army today. Lacey, you're unbelievable." Henry was always amazed at how many people Peter knew. At the moment he was grateful he had such a sociable friend, because until two days ago, he and Janie had been doing virtually all the work alone.

Within a few minutes the new recruits had joined the group already hammering away at creating Henry's version of Paris. Janie dumped the contents of the box on a canvas drop cloth and looked gloomily around her. The enormous room was a real mess. All the work, all the hours she and Henry had already put in and, to Janie's eye, the gym still looked exactly like an ugly, bare gym. It reeked of sports, not dancing. "It's impossible," she muttered aloud, as Peter walked by unspooling speaker wire to hook up the sound system.

"Nothing's impossible!" he exhorted, as he draped his arm comfortably around her shoulder.

"But there are only three more days, and this place looks like a tornado hit it." Her voice trembled. She was so tired, and she knew Henry was even more exhausted. By the time the prom rolled around she'd feel like sleeping, not dancing.

Woody popped his head in the doorway. "Hey, Braverman, Lacey, Barstow, Ford, where are you? You're wanted outside. Now!"

"What's up, Webster? We're busy." Peter gave Janie's shoulder a reassuring squeeze, and dropped the heavy spool of wire. "You'd better have a good reason for interrupting, or Henry will hang you from a basketball hoop by those dumb suspenders of yours." Peter punched Woody good-naturedly on the arm. The two boys sparred a minute, while Henry jumped down from the ladder and mumbled hello. He held a bunch of nails between his lips as he started moving the ladder toward the other side of the home team scoreboard.

"Union rules. You *must* take a lunch break now." Woody pulled the hammer from Henry's hand and took away the nails. "These don't count as lunch. Not unless you're trying to cure iron deficiency anemia. By the way, Peter, that was

124

the name of a band last week up in Philly, and they sure sounded like they needed vitamins." As he talked, he steered Henry and Janie in front of him out the door.

"But no one else is taking a break," Henry protested, with a gesture toward his volunteer crew.

"They all drift home before five, but you folks stay half the night these days. Supposedly working very hard," Woody quipped and tousled Janie's hair. She blushed, then gasped. Kim's Earthly Delights van was pulled up in front of the gym. She had spread a red-checkered table-cloth on the grass and was setting up a picnic.

"Kim, what's this?" Monica exclaimed.

"Lunch. On the house. My house, that is. Quiche, sushi, homemade apple pie. A choice assortment of — "

"FOOD!" Woody finished with a flourish. "For our starving artists over here. If Braver-man doesn't eat soon, he's going to turn into a profile."

Chapter
15

Phoebe banged her hand down hard on the piano keys. The sound was horrendous. "Griffin, I don't know what's with you today. You keep mucking around with the music," Phoebe burst out impatiently. "It's such a beautiful day. I could be out on the quad having lunch and not sitting around in this damp old theater growing mold on my skin. If you don't want to rehearse, we won't. After all, this was your idea, not mine." She glared at Griffin's back. He wasn't looking at her. He hadn't really *looked* at her all afternoon. Or only just barely.

Phoebe didn't care if she sounded mean and shrewish. Griffin was obviously in some kind of weird mood. Maybe he was getting temperamental. Temperament was probably a disease all rising young stars got. Temperament or not, as far as Griffin's singing was concerned, he wouldn't have a job if he sounded like this by the time of the afternoon full-cast rehearsal. She couldn't believe he still didn't have the simple tune to "Tonight" straight. That was the kind of song everyone sang in the shower perfectly. He acted as though he'd never heard it before. He was all distracted, and he kept forgetting the words, and flubbing the ending. For someone who considered himself a professional these days, he sure wasn't acting like one. And that scared her.

They had been rehearsing in the little theater for over a half hour. If necessary, Phoebe knew she could cut chemistry lab that afternoon to work with Griffin. No one would find them in the theater. And even if the security guard did, Phoebe would just say they were rehearsing for the upcoming chorale concert. Luckily her reputation as a good student gave her some leeway in the cut department: Everyone always took it for granted she had something important to do.

"Listen, I just can't keep my mind on it. Maybe we should quit. I'll head out to Maryville now. It won't hurt me to be there early to watch some of the other numbers." Griffin shrugged and walked over toward the darkened footlights. He stuffed his hands in his jacket pockets and stared distractedly out into the empty auditorium. His whole posture looked so sad, like one of those posters of James Dean in blue jeans they sold at the Movie Shack.

"Oh, Griffin." Phoebe sprang up and went over to him. She stood close beside him and rubbed her hand against the back of his neck. He felt so tense. "I'm sorry. I didn't mean to yell like that. But you've got to get over the hump in these

127

songs. You know you can sing them. Let's try it together. Just this one time." She stood up and reached for his hand. He hesitated an instant, then jumped to his feet and sighed. But he didn't take her hand.

"Okay," he said not very enthusiastically, and made his way over to the piano.

Phoebe inhaled deeply and followed him. She couldn't understand what was wrong with him this week. First of all she hadn't seen him since Friday night, though that had turned out to be a really special night for them. After the movies, Chris and Ted had dropped them at Phoebe's house. They had made popcorn and gone down to the rec room and watched TV until the last late show was over. Even then Griffin hadn't wanted to leave.

Since then, he had been tied up at the theater; rehearsals, costumes — Phoebe couldn't keep track of it all. Every day it was something different. First all weekend, but then Monday and Tuesday, too. He had called and canceled all their practice sessions. Phoebe had tried to prepare herself for the day when he'd concentrate exclusively on rehearsals out at Maryville. She just hadn't expected it to come so soon, and it left her with a funny feeling inside. Her afternoons seemed long and empty, though she had lots of homework, chorus, and singing lessons starting the next day, and then a commitment to help Janie with the prom.

That's why today was so special. He had suggested that he drop by school at lunch so they could practice on the old piano where they had sung their first duet for Woody's Follies. Phoebe had been overjoyed.

It would feel so special singing with him in the setting where they first met. She had even put on the same funky Boy Scout shirt and black calf-length pants she was wearing that day last fall. But he didn't seem to notice, he wasn't in a very nostalgic mood. If anything, he seemed irritated, distracted, and depressed.

As she sat down beside him on the piano bench she suddenly remembered. When he had called yesterday he had ended the conversation not with I love you, but good-bye.

"Okay, boss, where do we start?" Griffin rested his chin on her shoulder and looked past her at the music. "I'm having trouble with this one."

Phoebe obediently began to play the intro to "One Hand, One Heart." She missed the first couple of chord changes, her hands were shaking.

She willed them to be ready, counted a few bars, and began singing, "Make of our hands, one hand. Make of our hearts, one heart." Griffin's voice joined hers. Both of them sounded slightly flat, unsure, as if not quite believing what they were singing. Phoebe quietly put her hands in her lap. Griffin continued singing a phrase longer, before he noticed she wasn't accompanying him. He didn't look into her eyes right away. When he did, she quickly glanced down. She was too afraid to face him.

"I guess you're pretty nervous about this afternoon," she ventured quietly.

Griffin just nodded. He took one of her hands in his and massaged her palms. "I'm scared . . ."

He paused. Phoebe was afraid to breathe. She wasn't sure she wanted to hear what he was scared of. ". . . I'm going to make a fool of myself," he continued. "Nothing's going right." Then he added quickly, "I don't mean to lay this on you. But you asked me before to tell you — no matter how things were going. Didn't you?" He suddenly sounded so like a little boy, Phoebe wanted to hug him.

Instead she bit her lip. Her free hand toyed with the fabric of her pants. "Yes, I wanted you to tell me. But it's pretty obvious you're not feeling on top of things. What should we do about it?" As she spoke, Phoebe got the feeling they were talking about one thing, but meaning something else. She jumped up and paced across the stage, rubbing her bare arms with her hands. It suddenly seemed so cold and creepy inside the old converted chapel, as if winter had never quite left.

"I think we should try one more time," Griffin said, softly. "Let's try without the piano. Let's just sing it as a duet."

Phoebe turned around slowly. She knew what he meant. Maybe singing together was what they were really good at. When she had been nervous about singing for the Follies, singing *with* Griffin had dissolved the knot of fear in her stomach.

He reached out his hand toward her. Phoebe smiled. "Okay, boss. Let's try it your way."

They both leaned back against the piano. Phoebe softly hummed one note to give Griffin the right pitch, then they began. Griffin took her hand as they sang standing together, side by side.

It went better this time. They were both in tune. Their voices regained some of their old harmony. Phoebe looked up into Griffin's eyes, but he wasn't looking at her. He had his eyes closed.

Phoebe somehow managed to keep singing the words, but inside her heart was crying, Griffin, Griffin, where are you? Seeing him standing like that, a distant expression on his sensitive face, scared all the songs she ever knew right out of her. Griffin was in another world, and she was drifting to the edge of it. A sob rose in Phoebe's throat. She stifled it, but Griffin sang the last words of the song alone. "Now we begin, now we start, only death can part us now."

The silence after the last notes died away seemed to stretch out forever. Then Griffin dropped her hand. "Well, I'd better get going. I don't want to miss my ride." He hopped off the stage and stood looking up at Phoebe from the front row. "You really helped a lot, Pheeb. That went better this time, didn't it?"

Phoebe nodded.

"So when I sound like a pro this afternoon, I'll blame it on you. Next thing you know you'll be coaching and giving singing lessons yourself . . . to the whole cast." Griffin's voice was light and airy, and not very convincing.

Phoebe felt ridiculous looking down at him. She couldn't quite read his expression from here. She scrambled down beside him, just as he started down the aisle. She grabbed his hand. "Hey, wait a minute. Didn't you forget something?"

Griffin looked puzzled, then he shook his head. "Of course not, I thought you were walking me to the door." He tilted up her head and gave her a gentle, sweet kiss.

"Oh, Griffin." Phoebe pushed away from him, feeling very confused. "I didn't mean that. I meant the rehearsal. You promised — the end of this week. Well, that leaves tomorrow and Friday, and Friday's kind of bad because I promised to help Janie." She talked very quickly.

Griffin kicked his foot against one of the seats. He suddenly seemed aware that one of his Nikes had a hole in it. He bent and fingered the bare spot tenderly. He didn't look at Phoebe when he said, "I don't know. I didn't get a chance to ask yet. And tomorrow is so soon." Then he stood up and shrugged. "It'll be better by the opening, Phoebe. I mean rehearsals aren't such a big deal."

"To me they are." Phoebe pretended to pout, but a note of desperation crept into her voice. "Please Griffin, please let me come. That way I can imagine what it's like when you're working every afternoon. I can picture you there." She was almost begging. It made her sick, but she couldn't help herself. Somehow it was important to see inside Griffin's world. Maybe from there she wouldn't feel like she was drifting out of it.

Griffin finally met her eyes. He shrugged in a gesture of defeat. "Okay, tomorrow then."

"After my singing lesson."

"Won't that be too late?"

Phoebe pretended she didn't hear the hopeful note creep into his voice. "Not at all. No. I could be out in Maryville by about six."

"Okay. Then we'll have dinner at the break. Yes, Phoebe, that would be really nice if you came." With that, Griffin hugged her, and jogged quickly down the aisle, and out the front door. He didn't turn and wave good-bye.

The door didn't close after him and the sunlight flooded the theater entrance. A warm breeze finally made its way to Phoebe, reminding her no matter how cold she felt inside, spring was waiting for her outside. At least she'd see Griffin tomorrow. Out in Maryville she'd be able to look into the world Griffin was seeing behind his closed eyes.

Chapter
16

Phoebe leaned against a car in the Regional Theatre parking lot, trying to regain her sense of balance. Her world suddenly seemed topsy-turvy and she had a heady, unpleasant feeling she was about to fall off.

She took a couple of deep breaths and stared out across the rustic grounds. Twilight still lingered over the western mountains, and a big star seemed to be caught in the flowery branches of a huge magnolia tree at the edge of the lawn. It was the soft kind of evening that usually made Phoebe want to shout, and sing and dance, and hug everyone in the world. But tonight she only wanted to hug Griffin.

She knew as soon as she hugged him, the crazy, shaky feeling inside would go away. And then maybe she'd feel like singing again.

Though at the moment the very thought of ever singing again horrified her. That afternoon,

134

her first official singing lesson had been a total disaster, at least as far as Phoebe was concerned. She hadn't been able to concentrate on one thing Miss Spinelli said. Her mind was too full of Griffin. And her stomach was churning, as if going to see him out at Maryville was some new kind of audition. Phoebe had felt like she was about to try out for a role in Griffin's world.

Somehow she had mucked her way through a half hour of incredibly boring exercises. The teacher kept telling her to breathe, deep from her diaphragm. But Phoebe had trouble catching her breath at all. She was scared and upset, thinking about Griffin. And how he had sung with her, keeping his eyes closed.

When Miss Spinelli produced a copy of the *West Side Story* score and opened it to "Tonight" Phoebe almost started crying. She lied, and said she didn't really like the song. But Miss Spinelli started in with the introduction anyway. Phoebe managed a few opening phrases, then burst into tears. Miss Spinelli handed her a few tissues and acted as though breaking down in the middle of singing a love song was the most normal thing in the world. She didn't make a fuss at all, just told Phoebe she probably had had enough singing for one day. But when Phoebe left she felt like a perfect fool.

Another lesson was scheduled for the next Monday. She didn't know how she could ever face her teacher again.

Some guy started yelling inside the theater, his voice carrying out the open doors of the converted barn. A piano started playing the catchy

Latin rhythms of "America." Phoebe glanced up. That was a production number, but she couldn't remember if Griffin would be in it.

More than anything in the world she had wanted to watch Griffin rehearse for his first big role. Now she was too scared to walk in the door. Absently she trailed her finger across the shiny surface of the little sports car. Then she jumped, as if she had been burned. The car she had been leaning against was red. The license plate might as well have said Sarah.

Phoebe's large green eyes narrowed as she glared at the car. Of course, Sarah would be there, singing all those songs with Griffin. The thought of it made Phoebe sick, and angry. She squared her shoulders and marched through the door and into the back of the auditorium.

Her eyes widened. On stage the company was whirling its way through the last bars of "America." The choreographer was angrily yelling as they danced. But Phoebe couldn't figure out what he was yelling about; the performers looked terrific. She noticed Sarah was not in the scene. Neither was Griffin.

"Psst. Pheeb. Is that you?" Griffin walked toward the back row. Phoebe waited for him to throw his arms around her and hug her. He didn't do that. He put his finger to his lips and just squeezed her hand. His hand was clammy. He put his arm around her shoulder. His whole body seemed to be trembling.

"Nervous?" she asked.

He nodded, not looking at her. His eyes were fixed on the stage. The minute the dance routine was over, some people clustered in the front row started whispering to each other. On stage the choreographer singled out a guy and started yelling at him — something about being a klutz. Then the lights went up. Phoebe blinked. Griffin dropped his hand from her shoulder and folded his arms across his chest.

"So! Welcome!" he said, but his smile didn't look very welcoming, as if he couldn't figure out what she was doing there.

"Hi!" Phoebe mumbled, feeling like she had walked into a party no one had invited her to. "It's okay that I'm here, isn't it?"

Griffin nodded. "I'm just a wreck. I go on any minute."

"Do you want me to leave? Do I make you nervous?"

Griffin shook his head. "Don't be silly. You came all this way." There was an awkward pause. Griffin seemed to be waiting for something. He suddenly asked, "So how do you like it?" He gestured vaguely toward the rafters. "It's all I've got these days, but it's home," he joked feebly.

"Some people would kill to live in a place like this," Phoebe returned, almost as feebly. His home, she'd never thought of the theater as that before. Without an audience, without all the costumes, with stagehands banging away at the sets while the choreographer yelled at a dancer, the place seemed lonesome and cold. Phoebe couldn't imagine spending her life there.

Then a short man walked up to the footlights. "Neill! Carter! You're on next," he shouted.

"Uh, I guess this is it." Griffin's voice was shaky.

"Yeah." Phoebe suddenly didn't know what to say. "Good luck — or break a leg, or whatever."

He smiled, then started down the aisle. Abruptly he turned back. "You don't have to sit way back there. It's okay that you're here, really." Then he hurried toward the front and climbed the steps leading up to the side of the stage.

She sat down in the fifth row on the aisle and thought, stage fright! And a sympathetic smile crossed her face. You're a fool, Phoebe Hall. He's just scared. Scared to death. All at once she knew Griffin's distancing act that week had just been in her imagination. She squeezed her eyes shut and said a little prayer of thanks. Then the lights went down, and she sat at the edge of her seat and waited.

For a minute the stage was a big black hole in the darkness. Ever so slowly a pale blue light came up, bringing the dingy tenement scene to life. It was magic. Not even the quarreling voices of the lighting crew could break the spell. Phoebe wasn't at the Maryville Regional Theatre, she was back in New York; in one of those rundown neighborhoods she knew existed, but had never seen. And there was Maria standing in a simple white dress, her glorious black hair cascading down her slender back.

It took a second before Phoebe realized that the girl wasn't Maria; it was Sarah Carter. And it took her a second longer to realize that the proud, handsome figure next to her was Griffin.

The music started, and Phoebe almost cried

out, No, not that song, but she didn't. And Griffin and Sarah began singing the opening phrases of "Somewhere." Griffin looked edgy and nervous, and he didn't look at Sarah at all. Phoebe felt an unexpected flood of relief, followed by a terrible feeling of guilt. He was singing badly. She could hardly hear him over the piano, and she knew in the final production there'd be a whole orchestra. And she *did* want him to be as good as she knew he could be. Silently she began rooting for him, as he moved stiffly about the stage. Could this be the same Griffin Neill she had watched in Woody's Follies?

"Come on, Griffin, you can do it," she whispered. Instantly, she clapped her hand over her mouth, but no one seemed to hear her. She glanced quickly at the front row. One of the men with a clipboard was shaking his head.

On stage, Sarah must have sensed Griffin was in trouble. She reached out as she sang and took Griffin's hand; slowly she walked with him across the set. She turned and looked at him. Her brown eyes were enormous, even from where Phoebe sat. But Griffin didn't meet Sarah's glance, not right away. He seemed to be fighting something. But finally he glanced up, and their eyes seemed to lock. Even from where she sat, Phoebe could feel the electricity, the magnetism. Griffin's posture changed. Suddenly his voice rang out soft and clear, and his whole body expressed the tender yearning of Tony's tragic farewell to the girl he loves. Sarah and Griffin weren't themselves anymore, they had turned into Tony and Maria right in front of Phoebe's eyes.

Phoebe's hands clutched the arms of her seat. She wanted to run away, but she couldn't move. Griffin had looked into her eyes just like that during Woody's Follies. And afterward they had run off together to the old railroad station and shouted with joy into the wind. That was the first time in her life Phoebe had ever shouted as loudly and for as long as she wanted to. It was the first time she had ever felt herself. Then Griffin had gathered her into his arms and looked down into her eyes just as he was looking into Sarah's now. That was the night Phoebe and Griffin fell in love.

The last notes of the song died away, and Sarah and Griffin stood there stage center still gazing at each other, looking very much in love. The lights didn't come up. No one in the auditorium moved. Even the stagehands were quiet.

Phoebe stumbled to her feet and down the side aisle. No, she screamed inwardly, No! This can't be happening. It can't. It can't. By the time she reached her car she was sobbing. She got behind the wheel, tears streaming down her face as she struggled to get the key into the ignition. She didn't even notice which way she turned as she pulled out onto the dark two-lane road. She could barely see the yellow line through her tears.

A gas station loomed ahead. She knew she hadn't passed it on the way out. She was lost. But it didn't matter, she didn't want to find her way home. She just wanted to stay lost forever.

The station was closed, but the old phone booth just beyond it was lit up. Phoebe drove by, then pulled into a turnaround. She drove back and parked in front of the booth. She sat there a minute cooling her hot, flushed cheeks against the steering wheel.

How stupid could she have been to believe him. "Sarah's just my leading lady," that's what he had said. She could hear his strong, soothing voice in her head, the exact way he had said it. The way he had said in the movies, Friday, "Phoebe, I love you."

She broke down again and cried for what seemed like hours. Finally, though her shoulders were shaking, her tears seemed to have been all used up. She scrubbed her arm across her face. Only then did she notice she was still wearing Griffin's old sweater, the one he had given her to remember him by when he went to New York. She tore it off, though the evening was cold, and she was shivering. She crumbled it into a ball and tossed it into the backseat.

She climbed out of the car. Her head was pounding. Somehow she found herself standing at the phone booth, poking through her pockets for some coins. She didn't know where to go. She didn't know how she'd get home, or wake up tomorrow. Or how she would get through tomorrow without the hope of Griffin coming by that afternoon. She wasn't sure she even wanted to see a tomorrow with no Griffin in it.

But tonight she only knew she had to talk to someone. Her hands shook as she dropped the coins in the slot. The phone rang, once, twice, three times. "Oh, Chris," she whispered, her head pillowed against the window of the booth. "Please, please be home."

Chapter
17

"Phoebe?" a soft voice called. Some branches creaked further down the path. The voice called again, "Phoebe, where are you?"

"Here," Phoebe said very quietly. Then louder, "I'm over here, Brenda."

The leaves of the big rhododendron parted, and Phoebe looked up to see Brenda standing there. She had on her jean jacket and a short black skirt. Phoebe looked over Brenda's shoulder. No one was with her. Brenda had turned up alone.

"Chris really wasn't home?" Phoebe's voice was flat and disappointed.

"No, Pheeb, she really wasn't."

"Sometimes she does that when she's mad. Says she's not there. And makes you lie. I know that," Phoebe stated simply.

Brenda didn't answer. She sat down beside Phoebe on the riverbank and shoved something toward her. "It's cold. I brought you this. Maybe it'll fit."

"Thanks," Phoebe muttered, but held the thick pullover in her hand. A breeze stirred the water. The reflection of the park lamps rippled on the waves. Phoebe shivered. She inhaled sharply, then pulled on the sweater. It was tight, but the nubby knit was comforting. "How'd you find this place?" she finally broke the silence.

"Chris took me here once, after she had a fight with Ted. She told me this is where you two always came when you had to have a real heart-to-heart talk. So I knew where you meant." Brenda fell silent again.

Phoebe felt a stab of jealousy. This had been *her* special place to come with Chris, ever since they were kids and Chris needed to get away from everyone and cry after her mother died.

"So, do you want to talk about it?" Brenda's soft-spoken query startled her.

Phoebe shook her head in the dark.

"Pheeb, did something really bad happen at home, or what? You sounded so terrible on the phone. I mean, you don't have to tell me." Another pause; Brenda poked the soft earth with a stick. "But it helps. It always does. . . ." Then Phoebe wasn't sure she really heard the next words or imagined them. ". . . even if I'm not Chris."

"Oh, Brenda, I am glad you came. I really am," Phoebe burst out, then bit her lip. Talking about Griffin would make it seem more real. And she had a crazy feeling that she was living in the middle of some bad dream. Any minute she'd

143

wake up at home, in her own bed; the alarm would still be ringing. The river, the cool breeze, Brenda; Chris not being there when she needed her, the scene back in the theater; all would have been part of the same bad dream.

"You can trust me," Brenda said, as she gently reached over and touched Phoebe's arm.

It was as if Brenda had pushed a button marked Cry. A sob burst from Phoebe's throat. "Oh, Brenda, it's so awful. It's not that I don't trust you. It's just — " She broke off, and Brenda's arms were around her.

"Hey, it's okay. Whatever it is," Brenda whispered. "Just cry. You'll feel better. We don't have to talk." She gently patted Phoebe's tangled hair. "Poor, poor Phoebe," she whispered.

"It's so awful. I just want to die," Phoebe wailed. "It's — it's Griffin. The way he looked at her. Oh how could he, how could he do this?"

"Griffin?" Brenda shook her head in disbelief. "Something happened with Griffin?"

"Oh, Brenda, I can't believe it. And it hurts so much." She rocked back and forth as she sat and haltingly, through her tears, told Brenda the whole story.

"It's Sarah Carter. I knew there was something between them when I saw her in the car that day, and he denied it. I always thought I'd be able to tell what he felt, what he was thinking. He's different that way from — " Phoebe broke off.

" — from Brad," Brenda finished for her. "Yes, he is. Brad doesn't show his feelings easily. It drives me crazy, too." As Brenda confided that, the smallest of smiles crossed Phoebe's sad face.

She squeezed Brenda's hand. But Brenda kept talking about Griffin. "And I don't quite believe something's been going on between Sarah and Griffin. Are you sure it wasn't just being caught up in the role? Isn't that what's supposed to happen on stage?"

Phoebe pulled away from Brenda. "No," she practically shouted. "No, it wasn't that. I *know*. I sang with him on stage. I know what happens. It doesn't just end on stage, it begins. I can picture them now somewhere." She pounded the earth with her fist.

"Stop it, Phoebe. You're going to drive yourself crazy. You don't *know* anything yet. I saw you with Griffin on Friday. He looked tired, and out of it, but it was obvious he loves you. He certainly wasn't involved with Sarah then."

"Don't kid yourself." Phoebe was surprised to hear the bitterness in her voice. "Anyway, since he's been back. . . . Oh, I don't know. I thought it was perfect, Brenda, I really did. The spring, Griffin, loving someone so very much. But right from the beginning, it wasn't. Something's been wrong. He keeps not calling, breaking dates. I figured he was busy at the theater. But it's as if I don't fit in with his life. And now there's Sarah. . . ." Her voice trailed off miserably.

Brenda sat quietly a minute. "Okay, maybe you're right. I don't know, I can't know. You know what you feel. All you've got to go by is your feelings. But I know something about people. Griffin's not a liar. He doesn't hide things. Or even if he tries to lie, he's lousy at it. You know that."

145

"Yeah, I guess so," Phoebe admitted, remembering Griffin's crummy distancing act when he was in New York.

"So I think you should talk to him."

"Talk to him?" Phoebe gasped. "I don't ever want to see him again. How could I look him in the eye?" She paused, trying to picture not seeing Griffin again. Her heart stopped a second. "Anyway, why would he want to see me? He doesn't need *me* around anymore to rehearse with."

"That's unfair, Phoebe Hall," Brenda said angrily. "Griffin's not a louse. He's probably got lots of problems, like all of us. But he'd never deliberately try to hurt you."

Chapter
18

By the time Phoebe pulled the car into the driveway she had finally stopped crying. She glanced at the house. All the lights were out, except the one her mother had left on in the kitchen. It must be past midnight, Phoebe thought, and out of habit she quickened her pace. Not that being grounded now would matter, if her parents even bothered. They thought she had been out all this time with Griffin.

Her throat tightened, but she willed down her tears. She rubbed her palms across her forehead. But she couldn't erase the last thing Brenda had said when she walked Phoebe back to her car. The words kept going round and round in her head. Everyone makes mistakes. Even people we love.

"Phoebe," a husky voice called across the dark yard.

Phoebe's whole body tightened. She wanted to pretend she hadn't heard. She could run up to the house and pretend she hadn't seen the familiar shadowy figure get up from under the oak tree, and start toward her across the lawn.

"Griffin?" she whispered, then ran halfway toward the tree and found herself in his arms. Beneath her hands his strong muscular body was shaking. His kisses tasted salty. He was crying. But he kept kissing her through his tears. Then he was holding her so tightly she thought she would break in his arms.

I can't believe this, she said to herself. The next time she said it, she said it aloud.

Griffin stared at Phoebe as if he had never seen her before. "Oh, Phoebe," was all he said. Then he pulled her down beside him to the ground and cradled her head in his arms. "What's happening?" His voice was full of pain, as he rocked her back and forth.

Phoebe straightened up and forced herself to face him. She wiped her face with the back of her sleeve, her eyes never leaving his. She didn't know what to say. He looked as though he hurt so much — as much as she did. Was this what love did to people?

Griffin started speaking. His voice was low and weak, and the words came out in spurts. "I'm scared. I'm confused. I don't know what's happening with you and me." He took a deep breath and looked away from her, sitting back on his heels. He threw his head back and looked up at the dark, starry sky. Then he closed his eyes and shook his head.

"I came back to Rose Hill because of you. Because you are — and always will be — the best

thing that ever happened to me in my whole life."
His voice deepened with feeling. He looked up
at her and reached across the space between them.
His fingers traced the outline of her lips, then
strayed to her curls. Then his hand dropped back
limply to his lap.

Phoebe started to speak. "Griffin, you don't
have to say all this — "

His hand came up, as if to silence her. "No,
Phoebe. I *do*. Because since I came back it's been
all wrong. It's been glorious, joyous, wonderful
being with you. And all wrong at the same time."
His voice sank to a whisper again. "And I'm confused. And scared." He banged his fist on his
knee as he talked. "We're drifting apart, into
separate worlds."

"I know." Phoebe's voice was so quiet. But
Griffin heard her. He faced her again and took
her hand. For a minute Phoebe had hope. He
would tell her now what was wrong, what they
could do to make it better. Relationships weren't
easy, Phoebe knew that. There must be something a person could do to fix them, to make
them work again, to get back in tune.

"And I don't know how to get back to you,"
Griffin said flatly. "I don't know how to cross
whatever highway's come between us."

"Highway?" Phoebe repeated incredulously.
"Griffin, I'm trying to understand what you feel.
I feel the same way. Something's wrong, but I
don't think it has to do with highways, or dis-
tances, or worlds." Suddenly a note of anger crept
into Phoebe's voice. "Why don't you come out
and say what it really has to do with? Wasn't it

149

obvious tonight? At the theater? Everyone felt it. Even from the fifth row I could see it. The sparks were flying right up to the balcony. You were all turned on, Griffin. And it really showed. Come off it." Phoebe suddenly sprang to her feet. "You're the one who believes in always telling the truth, never lying. Taking risks. Haven't you got the guts to tell me that since your dumb audition a few weeks back, you've been dating Sarah Carter behind my back?"

Phoebe broke down, but kept on through her tears. "If you don't want me anymore, come right out and say so." Phoebe sobbed and started stumbling back toward the house.

Griffin scrambled to his feet and blocked her way. He grabbed her shoulders. "Let me go," Phoebe cried softly. "Let me go."

"No," Griffin said angrily. "I won't. And you're wrong. You've got it all wrong."

"Come off it." Phoebe tried to pull away. "You don't need to go through this act with me." She glared at him furiously, the tears drying on her burning cheeks.

Griffin stared helplessly at her, then dropped his hands to his side. "Okay. Go. Do what you want, but at least give me a chance."

Phoebe stopped halfway up the back steps. She closed her eyes a second. Had Brenda been right? Had there been some crazy mistake? Sarah was beautiful, sexy, and looked so romantic in her dress on the stage. What guy wouldn't get swept away? She turned around to meet Griffin's eyes. Maybe he would apologize. Or explain.

People you love make mistakes, she repeated to herself.

"I've never gone out with Sarah. I've never kissed her, except on stage."

He sounded like he was telling the truth. She sank down on the steps, propped her chin in her hands, closed her eyes, and listened.

Griffin paced back and forth as he talked, full of nervous energy. "It just all started with that trip to New York in Sarah's father's van — "

Phoebe's eyes popped open. "You mean the trip you wished I had been on?" she asked incredulously. "In Sarah's van?"

"Yes. I wanted you there to be with me, and to share my friends. I had a feeling it was important for you — for us. I don't know." Then Griffin stopped pacing and looked down at Phoebe. Everything about him suddenly looked so sad. "And that was when I started getting confused about Sarah."

"Sorry, Griffin," Phoebe interjected. "I don't get it. You want me with you. When I'm not with you, the first girl who comes along gets you confused. All winter in New York you never looked at another girl, at least that's what you said." Her voice trembled.

"It's true, Phoebe. Oh, I swear it's true." He was begging her to believe him. And Phoebe did. Part of her wanted to kick herself, but she believed him with her whole heart and soul.

"But now the first girl you play opposite to on stage, it's like iron drawn to a magnet. I don't get it. I just don't get it."

Griffin swallowed hard, closed his eyes, and

finally said with great effort, "I know. I feel like some clichéd theater joke: Young actor falls for leading lady. I didn't believe it, I didn't want to believe it. But, Phoebe, when I looked up tonight and you were gone, I knew you *knew* what had happened. I knew you *saw*. Oh, Phoebe, I didn't want to hurt you. Not like this. Not ever."

Phoebe sat stunned, staring at the bottom step. Then slowly she got up and looked up into Griffin's face. She wasn't crying. Her eyes were dry. She was all cried out. She felt very angry. "I don't believe you." She laughed a strange, hard little laugh. "I don't believe you, Griffin Neill. You don't want to hurt me. Well, what do you think you're doing now? How can you stand there and tell me this and expect me not to hurt?"

"Phoebe, please, believe me — " Griffin reached for her hand. Phoebe yanked it away and backed off into a corner of the stairs. She didn't want him to touch her, she didn't want anyone to touch her again. If this is what love did, she didn't want any part of it. Not ever.

"Phoebe," Griffin pleaded. "I would die if I thought my life had no place for a Phoebe in it." He paused, then added simply, "Can't we try to be friends?"

"Friends?" Phoebe repeated scornfully, then stopped herself. When had she gone through something like this before? Last fall: It was with Brad. Nothing in her life had ever felt so terrible as when he had looked at her with all that pain and hurt, and hatred on his face; because she had fallen in love with Griffin. And Brad swore they would never be friends again.

Somehow she knew she couldn't do that to Griffin. She just couldn't. And at that moment she realized she wasn't dead inside. She was alive, and being alive hurt like crazy. And she was still in love with Griffin. She always would be, nothing would change that.

Phoebe leaned against the porch railing, and said in a small, shaky voice, "I don't know, Griffin. I don't know right now. Maybe someday. Yes, someday, I'm sure we can — " To herself she added, When it doesn't hurt so very much to be with you.

She didn't dare look at him again. She ran quickly into the house and softly closed the door. Then she leaned her back against it and whispered, "Good-bye, Griffin." It sounded all wrong. So she said one last time, "I love you, Griffin," and flicked out the kitchen light.

Griffin stood in front of the closed door until the kitchen light went out and the light in Phoebe's room went on. He started quickly toward her ground floor window. "Oh, Phoebe," he whispered, "I don't want to lose you." Then he stopped. He took a deep breath and turned around. As he walked across the lawn, his shoulders were stooped, as if the realization that there would never be another girl like Phoebe in his life was too much for him to bear.

Beneath the streetlight, beside the bus stop he looked back. Phoebe's window was open. He wiped the tears from his eyes, and straightened his shoulders. He watched until the light flicked out in Phoebe's room.

Chapter
19

"Oh, Phoebe, here you are. I've been looking all over for you." Chris squeezed between the maintenance truck and the back wall of the old chapel. The first thing she noticed was that, in spite of the warm day, Phoebe was wearing Griffin's ratty gray sweater. Her new chintz suspender pants looked like they had been slept in. In fact, right down to her baggy crew socks, Chris realized, Phoebe was wearing the same clothes she'd had on yesterday.

She was sitting in the open doorway, legs drawn up to her chest, her forehead pillowed on her knees. The cold dark air of the empty theater blew across Phoebe's back, out onto the warm sunny driveway. Chris gave a little shiver. "Pheeb, are you okay? I mean it's past three now. You don't have to hide anymore. You can go home."

Phoebe didn't look up. Her eyes were dry, but her makeup was streaked and she had big circles under her eyes. And she didn't want Chris to see her looking like this. She felt last night that Chris had betrayed her. That was unfair, she knew it. But Chris hadn't been there when she needed her. Now it was too late; nothing Chris could say or do would bring Griffin back. "Yeah. I mean, I'm fine."

Chris pursed her lips. Because of Phoebe she had cut all her afternoon classes. She had gone crazy all afternoon looking for her after Cary Norton had mentioned on the cafeteria line that Ms. Barish had sent Phoebe to the nurse's office in the middle of the second period chemistry class. When Phoebe didn't show up around the quad by the end of lunch break, Chris had phoned her house, but there was no answer.

Just before the last tardy bell rang, she had run into Brenda, who didn't dare cut any classes, but who begged her to try to ferret out their friend. "Phoebe's in trouble. I haven't seen her all day. I'm worried about her. Look for her, I can't." That was all Brenda said before racing off to Spanish.

"Brenda said you were really upset." Chris crouched by an empty dumpster and tapped the handle of her tennis racket against the gravel walk.

Phoebe finally looked up into Chris's clear blue eyes. "So then you *know* what's wrong." She sounded sarcastic. She held Chris's glance a minute, then purposely stared at the dumpster.

"Not really," Chris said, with an edge to her voice. "Brenda believes in keeping other people's secrets. But I just was worried about you, that's all." She stood up and looked down at Phoebe. "Do you want me to stay or leave?" She gave Phoebe a chance to answer. A cold, hard look had come over Chris's face. "It's me, isn't it? You're still angry about the other day, in the ladies room. Aren't you?" Her voice rose slightly.

Phoebe took a deep breath and leaned back against the cool stone wall. She closed her eyes. Maybe it was her mood, but Chris was rubbing her the wrong way, Chris, the one person she could always turn to. Had she always been this self-centered? Suddenly Phoebe felt as though she didn't know who or what she could count on. Nothing — no one — was the way they seemed. Until yesterday, Griffin had loved her more than anything in the world. Until a couple of days ago, Chris had been the one true-blue friend who would stand by her through thick and thin.

One tear rolled out of Phoebe's eye and plopped on her arm, then another and another. She scrubbed her face with her sleeve, then reached in her sweater pocket for a tissue. It was already shredded and wet. She shoved it back in her pocket and buried her head in her arms.

"It's Griffin. It's over. That's what's wrong."

Chris could barely make out the words, but she instantly knelt by Phoebe's side and put a hand on her back. Phoebe recoiled from her touch and stared up at Chris.

"Go away. *Please*. I just want to be alone."

Chris rose slowly, unable to take her eyes off Phoebe's tear-stricken face. As long as she lived, Chris would never forget the wounded expression in Phoebe's beautiful eyes.

* * *

By five o'clock Phoebe wasn't in pieces anymore. She had snapped together like the parts of
Shawn's old plastic Legos set. A new determined
expression was fixed on her usually open, expressive face.

As she had told Chris, she wanted to be alone.
Being alone was the only thing that made sense.
She could see the rest of her life stretching before
her. Alone, lonely at times, but uncomplicated.
Counting on other people simply complicated
things too much, and made your heart ache until
you couldn't bear it, and wanted to die. Phoebe
didn't want to feel like dying. She wanted to feel
like singing again. That's what her life would
really be about: not about love, not about friendship, but about music. She'd become famous
someday. Millions of people would adore her —
from a distance, where she couldn't get hurt.

Shortly after Chris had left, she crept into
the bathroom and doused her face with water.
Then she did something she hadn't done in nearly
three and a half years.

She hurried across the quad, lost herself in a
wave of noisy underclassmen, and climbed into
a school bus. She didn't want to risk walking
home and running into anyone she knew.

When she got home, she noticed that her
mother's station wagon wasn't in the driveway.
As she ran into the house, she kept her eyes
averted from the old oak tree where Griffin and
she had stood last night.

A few minutes later she was on the city bus
heading downtown, the pink Saks shopping bag

resting on her lap. Today was the last day she could return the dress. She looked out the window, as the bus slowly filled up with late afternoon shoppers. Until recently, Phoebe had begun to think everyone in Rose Hill had a car. But lots of people didn't, it seemed — like Griffin. As the bus turned down Frederick Avenue, Phoebe suddenly found it hard to catch her breath. She should have remembered that the number ten went right past Griffin's house.

She forced herself to look across the crowded aisle. A little girl caught her eye. Phoebe smiled and waved and made funny faces at the toddler. She kept on goofing around, waving, until she was sure the row of old brick apartment houses where Griffin lived was safely past her.

Then she closed her eyes and rested her hot cheek against the window. When she looked up, the mall was just ahead. She climbed over the other passengers and got off.

"I don't believe it!" Phoebe murmured, as she marched through the mall toward the glittery entrance to Saks. She had walked this way a hundred times before and hung out around the big splashy fountain with the rest of the crowd ever since junior high, but she had never noticed the music store before. Maybe it was new. Whatever music she bought had come from the small shop next door to the Jenkins' bookstore in downtown Rose Hill.

She walked in the store. The walls were lined with shiny saxophones, tubas, horns, and clarinets. A couple of pianos and electric organs crowded the front of the small shop. But Phoebe made her way directly to the back. She scanned the wooden bins of sheet music, willed herself past the albums of show tunes and rock ballads, and felt in the pockets of her flowered pants. She pulled out the crumpled sheet of paper on which Miss Spinelli had written the name of some anthology of Italian songs.

Phoebe quickly found the book and almost died when she looked at the lyrics. How would she ever sing in Italian? When she found the English translations her heart sank. They were such dumb lyrics. Something about little adorable violets that smelled nice. Then she inhaled deeply, squared her shoulders, and headed toward the front of the store. If music was going to be her life, then whatever it took to become a musician, a good singer, she would do it. As for Italian, she'd have lots of time to learn it now: all those weekends, all those nights, without Griffin.

"Phoebe Hall!"

Phoebe looked around, but she didn't see anyone.

"Psst! Down here!"

Phoebe glanced toward the floor. Poking his head around the corner of one of the music bins, was Michael Rifkin. He was sitting on the floor, thumbing through some hardbound scores.

"Michael!" Phoebe exclaimed, confused that after her efforts to avoid everyone, she still had run into someone she knew. But she didn't really *know* Michael, he was a stranger to her life. He didn't even know there had been a Griffin. Maybe that's why she found herself responding to his warm smile, with a small, thin smile of her own.

159

Michael scrambled to his feet. He towered over Phoebe. He took the song anthology from her hand. "Don't buy this here," he advised in a conspiratorial whisper. "Try the store near the Albatross. You know where that is?"

"Sure. It's my friend Sasha's parents' bookstore. But what's wrong with this?" Phoebe had no idea why she was whispering.

"Too expensive." Again an exaggerated whisper. "You can get it there used. Everyone has to buy this book. Most people hate it. They sell it as soon as they can, it's a good two bucks cheaper there."

Phoebe startled herself by laughing. "Michael, we sound like we're plotting something very dangerous and very illegal. Thanks for the advice, though. Can we stop whispering now?"

Michael grinned. "Sorry about that." His deep musical voice rang out across the empty store. "I don't want the owner to get upset, but every penny counts, especially for musicians. That's why I work here sometimes."

Phoebe guiltily looked around the empty store. "Where's the owner?"

"In the back. I'm just about through for the day here." Michael stooped, picked up the scores, and briskly arranged them on a shelf.

Phoebe trotted back to the bin and replaced the book. "Well, I've got to get going myself."

Michael was doing something at the cash register. He seemed to notice her shopping bag for the first time. "Saks?" He raised his eyebrows dramatically. "Good reason to save on music." As he locked the register, he asked pleasantly, "Are you shopping for the prom? It's tomorrow, isn't it?"

The smile left Phoebe's face. "Yes. Yes, it is." Her voice trembled. She didn't meet Michael's eye. "Well, good-bye." And she started out the door.

"Hey, wait a minute. If your shopping's all done, want to come with me for pizza? Guido's, at the other end of the strip?"

Phoebe shook her head. "No. No, Michael. Maybe some other time. You see, I'm not shopping for the prom." She hesitated, feeling very lost and very embarrassed. She rubbed the top of one sneakered foot with the other, and held the pink bag in front with both hands. She didn't look up at Michael as she admitted in a small, sad voice, "I'm returning my dress."

Michael cocked his head and studied Phoebe for an instant. "Saks is open for hours yet. It's Friday, remember? Come on. I'm starved — for food *and* company," he urged cheerily. Before Phoebe could say another word, he yelled goodnight to his boss and guided her by the arm through the store. When they were out in the mall he steered her across toward the other side of the large fountain, past a squealing crowd of junior high kids, right into a brightly lit hamburger joint.

"This way," he said quickly, "you can keep your eye on Saks. First sign of closing, we rush you in."

Phoebe didn't quite know what to say; she felt uncomfortable beneath the bright lights, in front of the mirrored walls. Everywhere she looked she saw herself. She looked a mess. She was still wearing Griffin's sweater. She had pulled her hair into two pigtails, but her part was uneven, and curls were straying out around her face and down her neck. And she was all too aware she hadn't changed her clothes since the day before. Worse yet, she knew she looked exactly as she felt: a grimy, tear-stained little kid. To keep her eyes off her reflection, she studied her hands.

Meanwhile, Michael talked nonstop. At first Phoebe was embarrassed; she had trouble focusing her attention on his stories. But gradually she relaxed a bit. Whatever Michael was talking about, his voice was soothing. It was a beautiful voice, a deeper version of his mother's: musical, strong, full of expression. It was as if he was singing a story, not telling it. The sound of his voice gradually calmed her down. It was only when he finally lapsed into silence that she looked up, confused, feeling as if something was missing. He looked as if he expected her to do something or say something.

"I'm — I'm sorry," she stammered, looking away from his deep brown eyes. "I guess I wasn't paying attention. What did you say?"

Michael smiled his dazzling smile. He gestured to the table in front of Phoebe. Out of nowhere a mammoth burger with an order of fries had appeared on top of the D.C. landmarks placemat. Another plate was in front of Michael. He had already blanketed his fries with ketchup.

"Where'd this come from?"

"I ordered it. Remember?" He shook a scolding finger in Phoebe's face. Phoebe blushed. This was

162

how he probably talked to his little sister. "Come on. Eat up. There's a hungry look in your eyes." He was laughing as he said that, but his head was cocked to one side, as if he was studying her.

Phoebe bit her lip, then looked down at her plate. She had forgotten all about eating ever since her apple at lunch the day before. "I'm supposed to be on a diet." She smiled weakly and picked up a fry. She should be hungry by now. She bit into the fry. For a second she wondered how she would swallow it; there was such a terrible lump in her throat. She grabbed for some water and washed it down.

She tried another. This one went down more easily, even before the water. By the third fry she realized she was starving. By the time she picked up her hamburger she told herself, at least she wouldn't have to worry about fitting into her dress for tomorrow night's prom.

"Like I was saying." Michael continued his previous conversation, though Phoebe hadn't the slightest idea what he had been talking about. "The only problem with the school orchestra is it takes so much time. For instance, today was the first time in three years I got roped into something around school that wasn't related to music. Except, indirectly it was. My friend Peter Lacey — "

"Peter? You know Peter?" Phoebe mumbled through her burger. She grabbed a napkin and wiped her mouth. A happy smile crossed her face. "I should have known it. *That's* who you remind me of."

Michael laughed. "From the way all the girls

I know look at Peter, that's *quite* a compliment! And of course I know him. He's my best friend at Kennedy. We're music buddies from way back."

"Oh, I didn't mean the way you *look!*" Phoebe exclaimed, instantly wishing the floor would open and swallow her up. She hadn't meant to insult her new friend. "Oh, gosh, now listen to me. I mean, you remind me of Peter not because he's a hunk, but because he's so happy. And it has to do with music. I've been trying to figure that out ever since I met you. You see, Peter's a real friend of mine, too," she said enthusiastically. The more she looked at Michael the more sense it made. Peter and Michael. Right. The same joy, the same sort of bounce to their walk. Their way of listening . . . yes, that was it, Phoebe saw it. They *listened* to the world, the way artists like Henry Braverman looked at it.

Michael sat back in his seat and regarded Phoebe a second. The dead blank look was almost gone from her face. Her eyes were still sad, but her smile was very real again. He wanted to reach out and touch her just then, to make sure the happy smile stayed in place. But something about Phoebe today said Hands Off.

"So what happened today? I mean with Peter," Phoebe asked, demolishing the last bit of her burger.

"I blew up balloons."

"Balloons?"

"Yeah, millions of pink and green ones for the prom. His pal Henry Braverman and that great-looking girl, Janie Barlow, Barstow, whatever it is, are in trouble getting stuff finished in time.

Apparently, they'll be up all night. I would have stayed longer. I wanted to see what it looked like finished, but I had already promised to cover the store for a couple of hours this afternoon."

Phoebe guiltily poked at the crumbs on her empty plate. "I feel bad about that," she finally said. "I was supposed to help out today, but then . . ." her voice faltered, ". . . my plans got changed and I had to return the dress." She kept her eyes on the placemat. With her finger she traced the dotted line between the Washington Monument and the Lincoln Memorial.

Michael leaned back in his seat and stretched his long arms up toward the ceiling. "That's too bad, Phoebe, about your plans. From what I saw, the decorations are going to look spectacular." He signaled for the check. "But I think at night, with all the kids dressed up, and all the flowers on the tables, and the band, and Peter's whacked-out play list for the DJ, it'll be really magical. I wish I could see it."

Phoebe looked up. "You aren't going?"

Michael handed the waitress some money, shook his head, then threw his hands up in the air. "No date."

Phoebe was shocked. Michael was so friendly, and so incredibly good-looking. Almost every girl she knew would die to go to the prom with him. He didn't have the vibes of a guy who didn't have a girl friend. Like Woody before he met Kim, or Henry. He was as attractive as Peter, but in a different, more gentle way. Guys like that didn't not have dates. She didn't know what to say.

Michael looked over at Phoebe's pink shopping

bag. "Hey, Phoebe, since your plans fell through, and you already got a dress — would you consider doing me a favor?"

Phoebe closed her eyes; she had a terrible feeling what was coming next. She wanted to put her hands over her ears and not hear. "Michael — " she started to protest.

"No, really. You see, I've never been to a prom. Sort of the way the cards fell, I guess. And today, helping out . . . it just was so much fun. I felt a bit like, now don't laugh, Cinderella not getting to go to the big bash."

But Phoebe did laugh. Nobody looked less like Cinderella than Michael Rifkin.

"So maybe we could go together. You know, as friends."

"No." Phoebe shook her head adamantly. "Michael, it has nothing to do with you. Really, but I just can't. Not now." The whole idea was preposterous. The prom had been for her and Griffin. She would walk in with him, she had pictured it all. Dancing with him all night, then staying out forever. Being with the crowd of kids she loved, being alone with Griffin. It was all one thing. Without Griffin, Phoebe's prom didn't exist.

"That's too bad." Michael sighed. "I really did want to see it. Peter told me to come stag, but I kind of feel weird about doing that."

Phoebe was shaking her head no. How could she walk in with Michael? How would she explain Griffin's not being there?

"I thought maybe as a favor to a fellow musician. . . ."

Then Phoebe looked up. Michael was smiling.

He meant it, just as friends. She thought quickly. She tried to picture being home alone tomorrow night. It would be worse. Worse than homecoming. If Woody didn't have a girl friend, she might have gone with him. After all, Woody and Sasha had gone to homecoming. And so had Brad — with Janie.

"Okay, Michael, let's do it. Let's go together. It'll be really nice," she said hesitantly. "As a favor to a fellow musician," she added with a shy smile. It was the first time anyone had called her that.

Chapter
20

"Oh, it's all so perfect. I couldn't have dreamed a prom more wonderful than this." Janie sighed, then giggled. "You know, Sasha, I feel like Cinderella! There's been a wonderful fairy godmother in my life." She covered her face with her slender hands. When she peeped through her fingers at her reflection in the mirror, she still was wearing the same glorious champagne-and-gold dress. She should be used to Henry's miracles by now, but she wasn't. Anyway, that girl looking back at her couldn't possibly be Janie Barstow from Cincinnati, Ohio.

"It isn't a miracle, or a fairy tale. It's real. It's the real-life, wonderful Janie Barstow." Sasha squeezed Janie's arm. "And that dress is a masterpiece. You know, it looks like sunlight. It — " A foggy look came into Sasha's huge brown eyes. "Oh, it's a poem. I can feel it coming on." She rummaged frantically in the tiny antique satin bag her mother had lent her. "Not a scrap of paper. Not even a pen. Real writers are never caught dead without a notebook."

"Real sixteen-year-olds at their prom are!" Janie declared. The two girls stared at each other, then burst out laughing. "Anyway, you'll ruin my illusion. Just now, when you were dancing with Wes out there, you looked like something from *Gone with the Wind*, certainly not like a future investigative reporter for the *Washington Post* . . . or a bedraggled, starving poet."

Sasha grinned, and clasped her hands, and feigned a deep Southern drawl. "Tell me, do ah look like Miss Scarlett or the other one?"

Janie considered pale, lovely Sasha in her soft, full lavender dress: definitely not like Scarlett O'Hara. But Sasha was such a romantic, Janie lied a little "Miss Scarlett, and Wes looks exactly like Rhett Butler."

Sasha glanced quickly at her watch. "Oh, Janie, it's almost time." She gave a quick look at Janie's slender skirt. "You look perfect. In ten more minutes, you'll know the verdict."

Janie gulped. The whole idea of a formal march of the prom queen candidates with their escorts was terrifying. At the same time she loved the idea of modeling Henry's best dress yet. And he looked so wonderful himself, in that white linen formal outfit he'd put together after looking at some designs in *GQ*. She'd be scared inside, but she'd smile, and she'd be proud to take his arm and walk through the crowd.

Sasha led the way back into the gym. The

lights were low, and a slow tune was playing. For a second she didn't recognize Phoebe standing against the wall, talking to the tall handsome musician she had turned up with.

"Hey, Sasha," Janie bent down and whispered in her ear. "What happened? I mean with Phoebe and Griffin? Why isn't he here?" Her sweet face was full of concern.

Sasha debated with herself only a second. Obviously Laurie's gossip hadn't reached Janie, and Sasha wasn't about to put a damper on Janie's magical night. "Griffin? Something about the theater and rehearsals — they open in two weeks. He couldn't get away."

Janie eyed Phoebe skeptically. "She looks so outrageously beautiful tonight, but sad." Janie paused, then nodded. "I guess I would, too. If something happened with Henry, and he couldn't have made it. Who's the guy? He's awfully cute."

"Michael Rifkin. He's a musician. I interviewed him last year for an article we had to kill because of space. He's great. He's her singing teacher's son. Just a friend," Sasha added quickly. That part of Laurie's gossip she'd nip in the bud.

"Woody Webster, *you're* supposed to be one of Phoebe's best friends." Laurie had Woody and Kim cornered by one of the loudspeakers. "Are you going to tell me you believe that rot about Griffin rehearsing tonight? Some rehearsal. Only an hour ago I saw him cruising around with some glamorous girl, older than him, too, I bet — in a red Alfa Romeo. And believe me, it didn't look like what they were doing needed much rehears-

170

ing. Of course, if Griffin could see Phoebe now, maybe he'd *need* some consoling."

"Shut up, Bennington. You're always out to make trouble. Anyway, haven't you heard? You get more wrinkles from frowning than smiling." Woody grabbed Kim's hand and pulled her out onto the dance floor, just as the band blasted into a reggae number.

"Woody, I don't feel like dancing. Tell me, what's going on? Monica said Chris wouldn't talk to her about it. But something must be up." Kim tugged on Woody's gold metallic suspenders and pulled him to the other side of the room.

"Kim." Woody's voice was quiet. His hands fiddled with his gold lamé bow tie as he spoke. He looked directly into Kim's eyes. "I don't know. Phoebe hasn't said a word. At least not to me. But I know what girl Laurie's talking about."

"So it's true?" Kim gasped.

Woody tugged at his dark curly hair and looked down the gym toward Phoebe. She was smiling and laughing with her new friend. Still, in spite of her terrific dress, she looked all flat, like a balloon with the air gone out of it. Woody hadn't seen her dance all night, though her date seemed to know a ton of people, and Phoebe seemed to be enjoying meeting them. Still, the idea of a big dance, *the* dance, and Phoebe not dancing. Something was very wrong, Woody was sure of it.

"It sounds like Griffin's new leading lady — in the play out at the Regional. I don't know if Phoebe knows about it or not. I mean I don't even know if there's anything to know." Woody

171

sounded so miserable. He couldn't quite believe Phoebe wouldn't have confided in him. But maybe there really had been nothing to confide.

"Okay, let's not talk about it now," Kim said, smoothing Woody's shoulder with her hand. "And let's hope Laurie's just exaggerating. Maybe they were on the way to the rehearsal together. Couldn't that be it?"

Woody grinned. "Kim, that's what I love about you. I hadn't thought of that. Griffin doesn't have a car. He always needs rides to the theater. It's so simple, of course. As for that guy, I think he's a friend of Peter's who didn't have a date. It would have been a pity for Phoebe to waste that dress."

But as the music changed to a slow song, and Woody wrapped his arms around Kim, he closed his eyes and wished with all his heart that Griffin and Phoebe hadn't broken up. They had loved each other so much. He crushed Kim closer to him. Her dress was soft and suddenly felt fragile as a butterfly wing on her sturdy body. It was too scary to think that love like that might not last.

Chris and Ted brought up the rear of the prom queen procession. The applause was overwhelming, and Chris squeezed Ted's hand. She felt in her heart the cheers were as much for Kennedy's beloved first-string quarterback as for her. And, for the first time since the candidates were announced, she knew she was destined to win. She could feel the warmth of the applause. It was louder than for anyone else. Oh God, she didn't deserve it, she had let Janie down, and

Phoebe, too, somehow. Though Phoebe turning up here tonight had really surprised her. Poor Phoebe looked as though she would break down any minute. That Michael Rifkin was a nice guy, though. She wondered how they ended up coming here together. Someone reached out and squeezed Chris's hand. She looked over. It was Phoebe. Her eyes still looked all hurt, but she was smiling. And she mouthed "Good luck!"

The applause died down. Arlene, Mary Lou, Angie, and Megan stood smiling, holding bouquets of spring flowers. From where she stood, Phoebe could tell their smiles were forced. Probably even Mary Lou had expected to get the honor of being prom queen. Phoebe felt sorry for all of them. It must be tougher for the two seniors. This had been Megan and Angie's last chance. She wished she could have voted for every one of them. Then Peter Lacey announced into the mike, "Now for the second runner-up." He paused dramatically, his eyes going from Janie, to Chris, to Laurie, and back to Chris again. "One of the best-known voices around the quad, junior Laurie Bennington."

Laurie's hands flew to her face, and she shrieked. When her hands came down she was smiling, a forced smile. Then Dick Westergard reached out from behind her and squeezed her hand. Laurie started laughing and shrugged. Phoebe couldn't believe her eyes. Laurie actually looked at Janie and Chris and mouthed "Good luck." Though when she turned around holding the flowers tears were running down her face.

One fell and spotted her red silk dress. Laurie willed back the tears and struggled to keep her smile in place.

"Now, for the big one. The first runner-up. Of course, the one who isn't first runner-up is — "

Peter gestured to the crowd in the gym.

"PROM QUEEN!" everyone shouted.

"Hey, I didn't quite catch that," Peter teased, his green eyes challenging the audience.

The shout doubled in volume. "PROM QUEEN."

"What was that?"

"Shut up, Lacey. Get on with it," Michael's voice boomed across the gym. Everyone cheered. Phoebe found herself laughing. Michael leaned over and whispered in her ear, "Am I being *too* embarrassing?"

Phoebe shook her head vigorously, no.

"First runner-up is — Kennedy High's next student body president — Chris Austin."

The roar was incredible. Peter's voice barely was audible on the P.A. system. "Which makes our prom queen, *JANIE BARSTOW*."

The commotion on the stage was incredible. Janie screamed, and threw her arms around Henry, then Peter. Then all the other girls were hugging her. Except Chris, Chris stood apart. There was a stunned look on her face. Her hand was halfway to her mouth, as if she couldn't quite believe what was happening.

Phoebe silently thanked Ted as he took charge. He shoved the bunch of wild flowers into Chris's hands, and somehow pushed her toward Janie. Janie's face was wreathed in smiles and tears, and she looked like a real queen, holding the yellow and red roses, when Peter crowned her with the red-and-gold-tinsel crown. Somehow it went perfectly with her dress.

"Wow, she really looks like royalty!" Michael gasped.

Phoebe watched nervously, as she saw that Chris was standing back, not quite moving, not smiling. She looked like an icy statue in the middle of a bunch of laughing, screaming, nervous, and disappointed girls that now formed the prom queen's court.

Janie turned around, a purely happy expression on her radiant face. She reached out toward Chris. She was shaking her head, her crown slipping slightly lopsided over one ear. Phoebe could almost hear her voice. "I don't believe this. It's crazy. I just don't believe it." And Chris stared at her, her eyes looking blank. Finally, she reached woodenly for Janie's hand. She pasted a bright smile on her face, and her blue eyes glinted like glaciers, as she dipped into a curtsy with the rest of the girls.

"Oh, no!" Phoebe gasped. "Poor Chris." She knew that, although her best friend was putting up a brave front, she was crushed. Chris had never lost anything in her whole life, and now here she was, first runner-up instead of prom queen.

Chris knew she had to keep smiling until Peter rang down the curtain on the prom queen and her court. But as soon as the heavy blue drape descended and separated the girls onstage from the kids on the gym floor, Chris squeezed her eyes shut as she felt the tears threatening to spill forth. Taking advantage of the hubbub surrounding Janie as everyone crowded around to congratulate her, she made her way out of the stage door of the gym.

In the darkness, she stumbled away from the noises of the prom. She sought the quiet, cool depths of the pine grove beyond the parking lot, where exhaustion overcame her. She couldn't go on. She sank down at the base of one of the tallest evergreens and rested the back of her head against the rough, scratchy bark. Sobs wracked her body, and the tears she had held back onstage finally came gushing forth. Chris felt as though she had been kicked in the stomach as the full realization of what had happened sank in: She had lost. Janie, not she, had been elected prom queen.

She didn't know how long she had sat there when she heard the crunch of pine needles as footsteps approached. She sat up rigidly against the tree trunk and shivered. She didn't want anyone to see her like this. . . .

Then, suddenly, Ted was there standing above her. He sat down next to her and put his arms around her. Chris tried to pull away, but he held her tightly. "Oh, Ted," she sobbed, "just leave me alone. I lost . . . I'm such a loser."

"Loser? You're the winner, as far as I'm concerned. You yourself said how great it was that Janie got nominated, and now she's actually won — maybe the first thing she's ever won — and that's no skin off the nose of the next student body president. I mean, you proved that by the gracious way you congratulated her onstage."

Chris clung to Ted and didn't speak for a while as his words sank in. She still had tears in her eyes, but she got up slowly and began to brush the pine needles from her gown. She still felt kind of shaky and had to lean against the tree for support. Ted put his arms around her and brushed his lips against her soft blond hair.

"Oh, Ted, I feel so selfish. I wanted everything: student body president, honor society, prom queen, and Janie had nothing. I betrayed her, too. I told everyone I was voting for her, but then I voted for myself. . . ."

Ted laughed. "Hey, no big deal. Maybe it's not called being selfish. Maybe it's called having the will to win. That's just you, Chris. I should know, I'm the one who's on the losing side every time we play tennis. Right?"

Chris turned around and looked up at Ted. He looked so cute, standing there with a mock pouting expression on his face. She punched his arm playfully. "You better believe I'm a winner," she declared. "Next time we play tennis, I'm going to whip you six-love." Chris brushed away the last of her tears with the back of her hand.

Ted took her arm and started to lead her back toward the lights of the gym. Chris stopped. "Oh, Ted, do you think Janie noticed — I mean, I should have kissed her or something up there. . . ."

Ted drew her to his chest. "If you want to kiss someone," he said in a husky voice, "look no farther."

Chapter
21

Suddenly Phoebe couldn't stand it. She couldn't stand what was happening to people all around her — the hurt, the disillusionment — Chris, Griffin.

And then all the tears Phoebe had held back all night, threatened to spill out. She had to get out of here — now, fast. Before she made some awful scene and ruined Michael's evening.

"Michael." She tugged at the sleeve of his tuxedo. "Can we go now? I mean the excitement's over, and I just need some air, I think."

Then his hand was under her arm, and she let him guide her through the side door of the gym toward the parking lot. For the first time that night, she didn't tense up when he touched her.

As soon as they stepped outside, Phoebe pried off her shoes and wriggled her bare toes in the grass. Then she moved slightly away from Michael. They walked side by side toward the parking lot. He didn't touch her arm again. Phoebe didn't trust herself to speak, not just yet. The cool night air washed across her face.

All her friends, the couples so much in love, dancing with each other. The way Woody had held Kim that last slow dance, the way Chris and Ted had looked at each other when they'd come back inside. Phoebe bit her lip and rubbed her hand across her hot forehead in the dark. Maybe she was getting sick. That happened in stories, people died from loving someone too much.

Phoebe hadn't really wanted to dance at all. She did a couple of fast dances with Michael. He turned out to be an incredible dancer. She couldn't figure out how she'd never noticed him before. Except, of course, he probably never had time for dances. And all that bit about worlds not touching. Perhaps if Peter Lacey had given more parties, then they might have met before.

Phoebe glanced up the path. Two figures were silhouetted over by the corrugated tool shed at the edge of the parking lot. Instantly she recognized Brad's strong, square build. Phoebe couldn't help smiling. Brenda's slim figure looked even slimmer in her strapless, silvery dress. She looked like an Italian movie star. Brad's head was bent over Brenda's.

"So, do you want to go home?" Michael's voice was soft, he beckoned to her, to head down a different path. Brenda and Brad had stopped talking. Seeing them embrace like that by the side of Brad's car brought tears to Phoebe's eyes. She sniffed them back.

Michael stopped walking and asked gently, "Do *they* have to do with your change of plans tonight?" He pointed to Brad and Brenda.

"No," Phoebe stammered. "No, that was last year." Suddenly she felt ridiculous. "I guess that sounds stupid, doesn't it." She tried to laugh. Instead, she was crying, very softly. She tried to stop before Michael really noticed.

"No," Michael replied simply. "It doesn't sound stupid."

They walked toward the far end of the lot. Phoebe stopped to put her shoes back on. "Are you sorry?" Michael suddenly asked.

"Sorry?" Phoebe turned and faced him, suddenly struck by how handsome he looked in his tuxedo. It was a formal black one. It went well, somehow, with her dress. She had never seen a guy look so right in a tux. Then she remembered: He played real concerts, on real stages. He probably even owned his formal clothes.

"I mean about coming to the prom. Maybe it was wrong of me. To ask you — to do me the favor."

"No, Michael. I'm glad you asked." She sniffed. "I'm glad I came. Everyone looked so beautiful. And I got to wear my dress." She fingered the stiff, shiny taffeta. The tears welled up again in her eyes. "It was just hard, to see everyone I know, so in love." Phoebe leaned back against a tree. "I'm sorry. I'm sorry if I ruined your evening. You probably wanted to stay," she sputtered.

"No, Phoebe. It's not like that. I had a wonder-

ful time coming here with you. Really I did."
Michael paused a minute. Then he touched her
shoulder gently. Phoebe didn't pull away. She
leaned into his hand, and suddenly found herself
in his arms, crying. Michael stroked her hair, and
whispered, "Oh, Phoebe, who could ever do this
to you? You're not meant for this. Not at all.
You're such a happy person." Phoebe didn't know
what he meant. She only knew she'd never be
happy again. But she stayed in his arms until
she was cried out.

When her tears subsided, he said softly, "Come
on, Phoebe, let's go where we can talk. I think
you need a friend." Phoebe didn't protest as
Michael led her by the hand across the grass over
toward the baseball field. "This is where I go
sometimes to be alone — in winter, or at night."
He climbed up into the bleachers, helping her
negotiate the steps in the dark.

They sat there, shoulders touching, not saying
anything. Michael finally broke the silence. "This
guy, you really loved him?" He sat leaning his
arms on his knees. He was looking out across the
empty diamond.

"Yes," Phoebe began. "I really love him. I still
do," she whispered. Then she started talking. She
told him her story, about Woody's Follies, about
Griffin, about New York, about winter being so
long, and spring being so perfect. And then about
Sarah and Griffin's feelings for her. It all poured
out of her. It was terrible.

"I'm sorry. This is all so heavy. You came to
the prom to have fun. Not to hear this."

"I came to the prom to be with you," Michael

said simply and took her hand. "I only wish I could make you happy again. If I had my fiddle with me I'd play you a happy tune."

Phoebe started laughing through her tears. "I didn't know you played the fiddle."

"We all do . . . even my mom."

Phoebe sniffed quietly. She leaned her head against his shoulder. Music from the gym drifted across the quad. She closed her eyes. Oh, if only she could be with Griffin.

"You know, your friend Griffin, don't be too hard on him," Michael said suddenly as if reading her mind. "It sounds like he's a typical theater person."

Phoebe sat up and faced Michael. "What do you mean?" Nothing about Griffin was typical at all, Phoebe knew that.

"They're like that. They move on; from play to play, from role to role. And it carries over sometimes into their lives. I've met people like that. Musicians can be like that, too. But they aren't lying, Phoebe. Not at all. They are very deep and intense about what they do, who they're with. Then when the next play comes along, they pack up and leave all over again. And get intensely involved with something — or someone — new."

Phoebe closed her eyes. She sat very still and let Michael's words run through her brain. Yes. Yes, that was it. It was so familiar. It was true. The sudden magic between her and Griffin. It started during Woody's Follies, and it hadn't died as long as they were apart. No, Phoebe corrected herself, as long as Griffin hadn't had another play, another role.

She opened her eyes and looked out across the quad. In the distance the moonlight glistened on the river, and the lights of downtown D.C. made the starry sky all soft and hazy.

"Yes. Yes, Michael. That makes sense. It was like that with us." She paused. "Except that doesn't really help, does it. I mean, I still love him. I can't help who he is . . . what he does — " Her voice broke off. She closed her eyes again, as if looking at the soft spring night hurt too much. It was too much like last night. Twenty-four hours ago, she had been in Griffin's arms for the last time. She could still feel the places where he'd kissed her, how his hand felt against her arm, how he had held her. How his heart pounded beneath his soft old shirt. The tears started down her face again.

"Oh, Phoebe, don't cry," Michael whispered. He reached toward her face and brushed the tears away. She didn't move his hand away. "You're not meant for crying. You really aren't. You're like a happy song, Phoebe."

Then his lips brushed hers in the dark. It was a gentle kiss, gentle like the breeze that had just sprung up from beyond the river. And Phoebe couldn't stop herself from responding, hesitantly at first, then more and more passionately. Phoebe felt her whole body surge toward his, as he crushed her against him. She kissed him and never wanted to stop. She didn't want to open her eyes again. She just wanted to love him.

"Oh, Phoebe," he cried.

But inside she was crying, Griffin, Griffin.

And then he was holding her face between his hands and smiling at her. His smile was so wonderful, so radiant. But suddenly she was horrified. It was the wrong smile, the wrong face.

"Michael, stop. Please stop." Phoebe pulled herself away. Her heart was pounding, her head was reeling. "No, Michael. This is all wrong. It's wrong." She stumbled to her feet. Her knees were weak, and she could hardly catch her breath.

"But, Phoebe. . . ."

"Please, let's go. Now." Phoebe's voice was shaking. She didn't say another word until they climbed into his van. She sat far across the seat from him and kept her hands busy buckling her seatbelt.

"I'm sorry. I'm sorry for back there," she finally stammered. "I was confused. It wasn't you."

Michael started to say something.

"No, you don't understand. It wasn't you I was kissing. It was Griffin." Phoebe's courage failed her, she couldn't look at Michael's face. She couldn't bear to have hurt him. He was so kind and good. And, oh, at some other time, part of her seemed to cry out.

He simply turned on the ignition and started out of the lot. He tossed his longish hair off his face. He said in a low voice, "I'm sorry, Phoebe. I'm sorry I can't be Griffin. I guess I misunderstood."

Phoebe suddenly longed to take his hand, to try to make it better. But taking his hand, it would somehow be dangerous just then. "I can't help it. It's too soon," Phoebe whispered and looked out over the lights of Rose Hill. Griffin would be back from the theater now. She repeated to herself, It's much too soon.

They drove on in silence and Phoebe stared fixedly out the window. She was afraid to look at Michael. She felt so angry with herself, so cruel, so confused. Never had she let herself go so far on a first kiss. He must think . . . Phoebe frowned.

Michael had pulled up at the flashing light, then instead of making a left turn toward Phoebe's, he made a right, heading toward the interstate.

"Where are we going?" Phoebe gasped, suddenly afraid.

"I seem to remember that proms end with breakfast. So we'll have breakfast early." Michael turned toward her. His smile was a little subdued, but he looked her in the eye quickly, before glancing back at the road. He reached out his right hand. "Like I said, we're pals, we're friends. Crazy things happen prom nights. That's part of it, isn't it?"

Phoebe hesitantly reached out her hand, then returned his big wide smile. "Yes. I think we are that, Michael, friends. And crazy things are part of that. Aren't they?"

Michael nodded and flicked on the radio. He tuned in to one of those far away midnight A.M. stations and started humming along. It was a real hillbilly version of "Country Roads." Phoebe laughed as Michael started singing in a twangy voice. She found herself joining in. Her voice was weak and croaky-sounding, but it felt good to sing — especially riding in the big old van with him under the stars.

Michael looked across the seat. Phoebe had her head thrown back. She was practically shouting along with the music, a crazy smile on her tear-stained face. Her hair was half tied back with a bright pink scarf, blowing wildly in the wind.

He took a long, deep breath. She'd be all right, this Phoebe Hall. She'd be just fine. And watch out, Phoebe, he thought, one of these days you're going to begin to forget Griffin Neill. And you'll be happy again. And I'll be there waiting for you. No matter how long it takes, Phoebe, I'll be there.

Coming Soon...
Couples No. 10
SECRETS

Bill couldn't wait to tell Cynthia. "Someone named Charlotte Wodehouse turned in a poem to the literary magazine that is just fantastic. I was so blown away by it that I've been carrying it around in my notebook. I couldn't wait to show it to you."

Cynthia studied his face, she hoped casually. He didn't seem to be playing a game with her. "Charlotte Wodehouse?" she said. "I don't know her."

"I'd be surprised if you did. There's nobody by that name in the student handbook, and it's obviously a pen name. I wish I could find out who she is. There was something about her poem that fascinated me. This may sound corny, but I feel like I have a kind of bond with her."

Cynthia felt as if a hippopotamus had just sat on her stomach. She thought her heart would burst. He was beginning to be aware of the special feeling between them, too! Of course he didn't know that she was Charlotte Wodehouse, but her

187

poem had touched him just the way — no, far more than — she had hoped it would.

Cynthia was wondering how to tell him the truth, already feeling his arms around her, when he continued. "Part of it's mystery, of course. It's like getting a crush on someone you only know from seeing her in class. You know you like her looks, and you can imagine that her personality is pretty much any way you like."

"Until you meet her," Cynthia pointed out.

"Right. She might turn out to be a total witch."

"Then maybe you shouldn't try to meet your mystery poet."

He shook his head. "No, someone who has that kind of beauty in her has to be special. You know, Cyn, I'm really lucky to have you as a friend. Who else could I talk about such crazy stuff with? Falling in love with someone after reading a poem she wrote. Most people would think I'd gone right off into the twinky zone! But you understand, and you don't think I'm a flake because of it. That's very important to me."

"Bill — " she began, then closed her mouth. How could she confess to him now? He would be sure that she had deliberately tricked him into talking like this, and he would hate her for it.

He misunderstood her silence. Clapping her on the shoulder, he said, "I didn't mean to embarrass you with all the mushy stuff. Friends forever, right, kiddo?"

"Right," she said with a sinking heart.